Nicholas Stafford-Deitsch was born in the USA but he has lived in England since childhood. He attended Oxford University and worked briefly in merchant banking and venture capital. *The Toucan Feather* is his first published novel. It introduces a timely philosophy that is explained in tocamu.com.

Acknowledgements

I would like to thank the many people who have kindly read and commented on the manuscript over the years ... without their suggestions and encouragement I would never have completed my novel! The same is true of the illustrations – I am not a trained artist but I undertook this rewarding challenge when the first draft of the manuscript was completed. People have asked me where my inspiration comes from. Sometimes images have jumped into my head, on other occasions I have gone to sleep to waken with a design that I then commit to paper; or I've closed my eyes and let the images come to me. When I've struggled for ideas, I've used reference books and the internet ... I even based a picture on an advert I saw in a national newspaper for a UK brewery company! On occasions I've copied freehand photographs quite closely; on others I've embellished them beyond recognition.

THE TOUCAN FEATHER

WRITTEN & ILLUSTRATED BY
NICHOLAS STAFFORD-DEITSCH

tocamu

First published in 2010 by Tocamu Publishing
Copyright © 2010 by Nicholas Stafford-Deitsch

A CIP catalogue record for this book is available from the
British Library

ISBN 978-0-9565812-0-4

For Toby and Lara

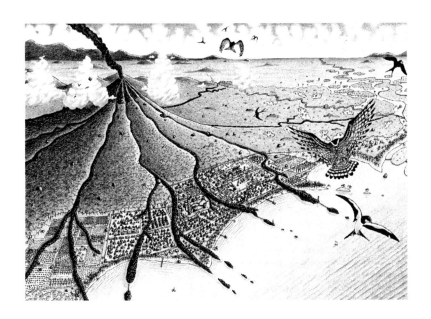

THE SILVER CONCH

Miago lived in a house of bamboo and palm. On waking he would listen to the whoosh of the surf and the tinkle of his shell curtains because they revealed the mood of the ocean. A southerly breeze scented the boy's room with bougainvillea but warned of strong currents; when he smelt hibiscus he knew the wind had swung to the north, which brought calm swells to the reef and nectar moths to his garden. Outside, a patchwork of coarse grass ended at a wall of coral rubble which was where the forest began. The beach was dotted with fallen coconuts and criss-crossed with crab tracks. A line of dugout canoes rested on the sand, their curved prows pointing at the vastness of the ocean where the boy was now swimming with the morning current.

Miago had heard rumours about this place, because the mollusc that poisoned fish and the fungus that tainted crops were unknown here; even the typhoons that ravaged the distant islands never came ashore. Despite these blessings, no one described it as paradise because his home rested in a shadow that was cast neither by the forest uplands nor by the old tower that reached skyward like a broken finger. Darkened and still, the house crouched like a mouse caught in a storm, beneath the rising slopes of a great volcano.

Miago sliced through the waves in search of shells. Ignoring his tiring muscles, he swam quickly in the cooler, deeper water that mixed strange shapes and colours with the promise of greater reward. Coming to a patch of dead reef where a stone column lay gripped in a fist of lava, he remembered the stories the old ones told of the eruption: how the reef choked beneath a blackened sky and the fish moved away. They said it took ten rainy seasons to wash the ash from the trees, ten more before they fruited again.

Miago glanced ashore at the crumbling palace and wondered what life had been like before everything changed. He felt a tingling and the colours around him brightened. "Not now!" he shouted. Because he knew he could drown if he had a vision when swimming.

In an instant he was transported to a place of soft light and chattering parakeets. An emerald hummingbird hovered beside him. "Why aren't you afraid of me, little bird?" he asked. He walked down a broad avenue shaded with palms. There were elegant houses with doors of carved mahogany fronted by bright, ordered gardens; in one, lemon-winged butterflies danced over a fountain of bronze dolphins. The sound of laughter drew his attention and he stopped at the steps of a great temple where wide-eyed children fed fruit to black-eyed lemurs. Though his vision had opened a door on the past, Miago felt only sadness because he knew he was separated from the city of his ancestors by more than time.

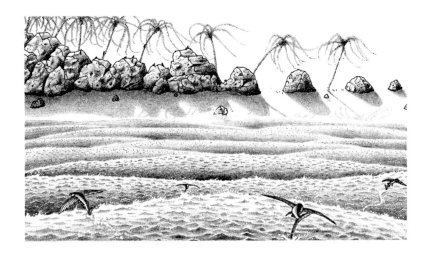

The vision ended as quickly as it had started and now he was floating above a scattering of broken pottery. What had triggered it? A shape on the sand caught his eye and he dived. Down he swam, fighting against the pull of the current. He jabbed the claw-stick, snagging the shell, before thrusting upwards to join his bubbles that danced on the mirror of the ocean's surface. Treading water, he slipped the conch shell into his bag and began searching for more. The seabed was deeper here and, as he drifted with the current, it dropped quickly away.

He checked his bearings; offshore, a bank of cloud shrouded Offal Rock. Onshore, boulders littered the sand. His pulse quickened because he pictured T'lu-i singing as she carried the baby turtles to the surf. Were the young monkeys watching her from the edge of the forest? He felt the heat of the sun on his face, which would soon drive her home and the monkeys into the shaded tree tops.

"What have you found?" he asked a circling seabird. It swooped and, on long, elegant wings, it carried its victim away. Miago wondered if he could reach the bottom here; he knew that one dive in search of shells wouldn't hurt. He went down quickly, pushing hard. Away from the reef he felt small and vulnerable but the challenge excited him – he was nearly a man and he'd prove it. *Keep going Miago, show no weakness!*

The beams of sunlight faded with depth. Another twenty strokes took him into a dimmer, cooler zone, a grey-blue world which the light that danced in the shallows struggled to enter. He spotted a drab starfish that would have shone red on the surface.

The pounding grew in his temples, but he stayed because the stillness held him. When his chest tightened and the first spasms came, he ignored them and went deeper. Ten thrusts later and Miago was studying the seabed that stretched away into the watery mist. There were no fish; he saw no coral or weed. He was about to return to the surface when a flicker of light blinked on a shape far away.

It could have been anything but Miago dared to wonder because, like everyone, he had heard the stories. He remembered the old man who swore he'd seen a bright conch shell, the trembling of his voice when he said it shone like silver.

Miago drove himself on, marvelling at the pool of light the shell threw on the sand. A few more strokes and he lined up the claw-stick. Giddy with excitement, he thrust down but either his aim was off or his eyes betrayed him because he seemed to stab straight through it. Miago jabbed again but he was rewarded with only a puff of sand. The pounding blackness was blurring his vision now and a desperate search failed to find the shell. With a silent shout of disappointment, he kicked for the surface. His only thought was of air.

Miago's first strokes were powerful. He pretended there was no danger but when he looked up, he knew he was too deep. His jaw tightened. *What if I drown and they don't find my body? Will they say I escaped and lock my family in the body cages?*

Miago's chest was heaving and a screaming filled his ears as he fought the urge to open his mouth and breathe. When he saw how the light reached for him like a flickering hand, he guessed he was halfway. He swore he'd never dive this deep again as he demanded one last effort from his tortured body. But he knew he wasn't winning as the terror of drowning grew. Panicking, he struggled to remember which way was up as his jerking limbs slowed and everything blackened.

Gripped by the current he drifted like a clump of weed. As his eyes closed, an image flashed across his mind. It was Cufu, his lost brother.

The grey shape that twisted from the gloom arched under the boy's body and jolted him upwards. He was dimly aware of a streaming brightness as the dolphin thrust him towards the surface. A surge of energy filled Miago and he burst through the waves gasping for air and coughing, dragging in air again and again as he filled his aching lungs.

Slowly his senses returned and the pounding in his ears receded. Squinting into the sunlight he tasted the salt of the ocean. Though he felt strong again, there was bruising in his chest. He coughed and spat something out, turning so that he wouldn't see it. Despite the pain he was smiling because it was years since anyone had seen a silver conch and he, Miago, had found one. A splash made him turn. The dolphin was already arcing skyward in a second jump. He saw the grey of the flanks and the water that streamed from the slick body. What surprised him was its size: it was only a young dolphin. He heard its throaty clicks. To the boy they sounded like laughter, and he laughed too. He turned on his back and swam for shore with the dolphin at his shoulder.

Miago was alone when he entered the shallows. Far away the dolphin erupted from the surface. In one great leap it climbed skyward, its twisting body crashing back in an explosion of bubbles. As the surface calmed, he shouted, "Thank you, little dolphin, you saved my life. I pray the ocean always protects you!"

Miago's thoughts darkened when he swam into the shadow of the volcano. He studied the blackened slopes and whispered, "Great Goddess Banakaloo-Piki, you took your revenge. Why won't you forgive your people?" As his feet touched the sand, his thoughts returned to the silver conch. He liked the idea of boasting about it. But would anyone believe him? What if word reached *them* and he was summoned before the Supreme Council? Then there was the dolphin – its beauty and energy and how it had come from nowhere to save him. If he told his parents how close he'd come to drowning they might forbid him from swimming outside the reef. His days would then be spent hunting for stingrays on the sand-flats and searching for the buried valuables of his ancestors. As the water dripped from his body, he made a decision: he would keep the story of the silver conch and the dolphin to himself.

Miago adjusted the bulging sack as he approached the market that shimmered in the heat. Moving from stall to stall he watched the sparring between the buyers and sellers. He listened to the shouts of one trader, studied the wares of another and smiled because he knew he was now strong enough to handle a man-sized claw-stick. With it he'd prove he was the best diver and that meant more money.

Miago pictured the claw-stick's design and he wondered whether he should try something new. He thought of the bamboo thicket in the jungle, hoping no one had taken the poles to use as roof frames. He rubbed the stubble on his chin as his mother's words returned: *now that you've grown into those huge feet, the other divers won't stand a chance!*

It had been a long wet season and the soil was still soft underfoot. Miago cursed. Why did the Great Goddess punish his people with rain fever? With less rain now, the humidity would drop and the sea breeze would make sleep comfortable. Better still, there would be fewer mosquitoes. Only yesterday his sister had risen from her sick bed but poor Cufu had not been so lucky. The prayers, the offerings and the healer's visits were fresh in Miago's mind. Despite them, little by little Cufu had slipped away. A tear worked down Miago's cheek as he wondered what sort of man his brother would have become.

He wiped his sweating brow, remembering that he was commanded to thank the sun for its heat but it felt so hard to obey. He recited another teaching, "The Great Goddess of the Volcano sends clouds to shield the sun to remind us of her anger.

If we displease her, she'll hurl molten rocks on us again and turn day to night. We must worship a black sun to remind us of our ancestors' follies."

With luck there would be many taku-aura this year. Miago had heard the elders talking of the old days when the schools of fish stretched as far as the horizon; of the countless sea birds that wheeled above them and the dolphins that drove them into the waiting nets. It had been a time when his people had no word for "hunger". There were stories about the sacks of gold, the strange looking merchants and the wagons that carried the dried flesh away. With a sigh Miago studied the temple built on that wealth, praying those days would return. He remembered the vision – the hummingbird, the laughing children, the lemurs. Now the temple was a broken relic from a time his father refused to discuss. He heard something that may have been the breeze playing on the cracked columns or the rasp of thorn on stone. The temple seemed to whisper to him and in a soft, dry voice it begged him to challenge the Goddess of Fire and Thunder that lived in the volcano.

"No, it's too dangerous!" he shouted, causing people to turn and stare. *Visions! Voices in my head! What's wrong with me?* He pushed these thoughts away as he wondered if T'lu-i would be in the market today. He pictured her face, her eyes and the joy in her smile. The shells felt lighter now and his footsteps quickened.

Someone barged into Miago and he spun round, ready to complain. Instead he jumped back not from the hurrying soldiers, though their swords were drawn. It was the cloaked and hooded figure they escorted that caused the boy's fists to tighten.

The crowd parted as the group stopped at the temple where a man slept on a bed of weeds, his head resting on the carcass of a butchered shark. The tattered clothes were stained and dirty, hairy feet spilled from broken sandals. Content in his dream, his snores resounded like gurgling thunder.

Slowly the hooded figure drew a stingray tail from the deep folds of his cloak. He flexed it and hissed, "He knows he can't sleep here. Or sell his rotting fish." He tapped the man but there was no movement. "He's drunk again." The crowd fell silent as the whip rose; they winced as it fell.

The man woke screaming as the first blow slashed his face. He threw his arms up in defence. The crowd now laughed as he struggled upright, swaying, trying to focus. He turned to run and this time the whip lashed his buttocks. He waved his fists and bellowed defiance before bounding up the temple steps, cursing as he wrenched at the door.

The hooded figure sneered, "You're wasting your time, Monkey Blood. Have you forgotten? That door is now locked."

Monkey Blood turned and Miago saw the purple welt across his cheek and the fury in his tear-filled eyes. "Who dares attack first?" he roared at the soldiers. Retreating, his voice now trembled, "You, you all come at once?"

Miago looked away as he was overpowered. The last words he heard were: "Bind him tightly and throw him in his usual cell."

Moving on, Miago came to a stall where a man held up a brown mass that dripped ink and buzzed with flies. He glanced at Miago. "Your father said you're always late." Then, addressing the crowd, he bellowed, "Buy your fresh octopus here!"

Miago watched in silence until the man spoke again. "What took you so long? I thought the Moroks had captured you!" He was staring at Miago's sack. "I could have sold fifty conchs by now! How many do you have?"

"Twelve," he said. "But I must take two home."

"Twelve at this time of year? That's good. Put them next to Six Toes's fish."

The bulging eyes of a mouse fish stared blankly at Miago. Beside it lay a mound of spotted soldiers and striped snappers. There were red-gilled grunts and blue-tailed tangs; marbled eels and even a queen fish. He saw sardines and glass minnows but it was the huge grouper he studied the longest, as he stared into the cavern of its mouth.

"Why are their mouths locked open?" Miago asked.

"Six Toes' fishing potion does that."

"I wish I knew his secret."

"So do all the fishermen. What I know is he throws it in up current and waits. They say he'd rather die than reveal how it's made."

"But how could *he* have made it? He has no brain!"

The man laughed. "Then he must have paid someone."

"I've heard the other fishermen have potions that work quite well. Soon we'll have all the fish we need."

"Next time you go fishing bring me some stingray tails. They sell well around here."

"How many?"

"Ten. Oh, by the way, that girl you like wants a silver conch. Can you spare one?"

He didn't miss a beat. "Only one?"

"In thirty years I've seen everything the ocean produces but never a silver conch. Catch one and I bet she'd pay a fortune for it!" Under his breath he added, "And find a nice way to thank you."

Miago blushed as he opened the sack. "Fresh conch for sale!" he shouted. It was soon empty.

The throng of people had moved into the body of the market and Miago could see that trade was good today. The piles of mangoes, bananas and plantains had gone and the cloth seller who had hung her patterned fabrics on the bamboo railings was smiling. The fruit bat cages and crab traps were empty; even the old woman with the angry face was quietly counting her money.

When Miago had been paid, he thought of T'lu-i. Her father owned many of the stalls so he didn't know where to look for her. He would start at her favourite: the one selling crystals and shells.

Miago had taken only a few steps when he found his path blocked by a man. He was thin and pale-skinned; he carried a stick but it didn't look as if he needed it for support. His tunic was ragged. When Miago saw that his legs were spattered with mud he knew he must have walked through the forest but his sandals were clean and looked new. The man's cheeks were round and soft, as if the food he ate nourished only his head. The stubble matched the grey of his calm eyes.

The man smiled warmly. "I wonder if you could help me,

young man."

Miago sensed he'd have to look for T'lu-i later.

"They told me you might have some spare conch. I don't have money, but I can pay in other ways."

Miago studied him carefully. "I'm sorry," he said. "I've two left but they're for my family."

The stranger smiled again and Miago found himself smiling too.

"I understand. Thank you for your time." He turned and walked away.

Miago couldn't resist so he chased after him and tugged his sleeve. "If you don't mind me asking, how else would you pay for them?"

"There are many ways we can pay." He held out his hand. "Some call me the Teacher."

"We don't need more teachers here."

"Indeed? Let me ask you something. Why does every adult have a scar on their forehead?"

This man has obviously never been here before. "So that people know what we believe in. It's been our custom since –"

"A new custom? And why has the Temple of Light been painted black?"

Perhaps he has been here? "It's only called the temple now and they painted it black when they locked it."

"But why?" the stranger persisted.

Miago didn't answer as he gazed over the man's shoulder.

"I see that you've more important things on your mind. Perhaps our paths will cross again."

Miago soon forgot him. Quickly he cut through the market. He dodged behind a palm trunk and used a line of carts for cover. It would be worth it to hear T'lu-i's laugh when he tickled her.

He was close to T'lu-i when she spun round. Miago froze, hoping his smile would save him.

For a second she looked surprised. "Were you sneaking up on me?"

"No! I was going to the knife seller. I …"

"Don't stand there blushing! Come and help me."

The rest of the day didn't feel like work because he was near her. He had stolen glances and found excuses to brush her arm. And he liked the way the other boys stared.

"I almost forgot," T'lu-i said. "I have something for you." She held out her hand. "Careful, it's sharp."

"What is it?" Miago asked.

"A fish hook! But it's metal."

"It'll rust in a day!"

"Father says it will last for years and those spikes will stop it falling out of the fish's mouth."

Miago felt the tip. "I'm happy with my bone hooks. Where did it come from?"

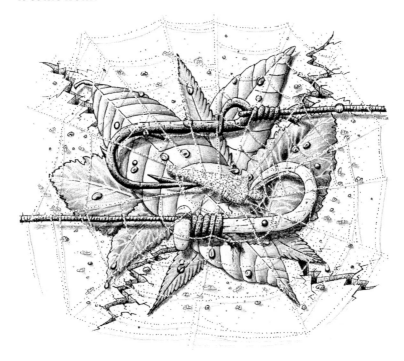

"He traded it with an outsider. Twenty hooks for a pair of sandals. He's already doubled his money."

"Sandals? Oh, *him*. But the ocean eats metal. Your father won't be so pleased when the fishermen demand their money back."

"No one has a better eye for what sells. You could learn a lot from him."

Miago considered this. "You know what they say about him?"

"What?"

"Even the sharks go to him for advice."

Her eyes sparkled. "Are you mocking him?"

He feigned terror. "No. No. I promise."

Now she was giggling. "Because if you are … I'll have to punish you."

"Oh?"

T'lu-i's hand shot out to tickle him but he grabbed her wrist. She moved closer without looking away. "Someone help. He's attacking me!"

Miago dropped her arm and stepped back. He was blushing again. As they stared at each other, he heard the thumping of his heart. "I'll let you know if I catch anything with it."

She giggled again. "I can't wait."

The heat had left the day and Miago was polishing and arranging the unsold shells to their best advantage. He saw how T'lu-i would catch someone's eye, smile and engage them in conversation as she invited them to inspect a shell or a crystal. He noticed how interested she seemed to be in her customers, how she flirted with the men, how charmingly she negotiated with the women. Her father had taught her well. But he felt more comfortable standing back and letting her do what she was good at. She was talking to a young man. "If you really want to impress her, buy her a crystal that matches the colour of her eyes. Women notice things like that."

Miago was lifting a triton shell when the stranger he'd met earlier approached the stall. The shell slipped from his fingers and shattered at his feet. Miago was cursing as the man spoke. "There's a saying: break a triton, end a dream."

The shell was forgotten because the man's words had stirred a memory Miago had pushed to the back of his mind. He felt the sickness in the pit of his stomach; there was wretchedness in his voice. "You don't need to remind me."

The man looked confused.

Miago saw that T'lu-i had stopped smiling and she was watching the man closely. He steadied his voice. "The ceremony is coming. It's when we must make our Life Choice."

The stranger knelt to collect the fragments. "May I take these?"

T'lu-i nodded. "Yes, we can't sell them."

Miago was about to speak but T'lu-i was quicker. "What will you use them for?"

"Oh, I'll think of something. I like to make things and shells are good for decoration. Ground and polished, nothing is whiter."

"Promise to show us what you make," said T'lu-i. "Perhaps we can sell things for you."

The stranger hesitated. "I should introduce myself. They call me the Teacher."

"What is it you teach?" T'lu-i asked.

"I teach people to ask questions."

Miago shrugged. "Here we only learn answers."

"Anyway you can't call yourself that around here," T'lu-i warned.

"Oh?"

"Our teachers are chosen by the Men of Knowledge," she explained. "Anyone else who teaches is thrown in prison."

"I see. So what would you like to call me?"

"You said you make things," T'lu-i said.

"Yes?"

"Would you mind if we called you … the Maker?"

"Will *that* name get me thrown in prison?"

Every year, Miago knew, brought more laws. Sometimes, when he lay awake, the still of the night was broken by the cries that drifted from the prison. "Anything can get you locked up here."

"I see. Well then, the Maker it is."

Miago and T'lu-i introduced themselves. Miago added, "These are our names for now. We don't know our adult names yet."

"Adult names?"

"When we're born we're given the traditional names of our ancestors. After the ceremony, when we've made our Life Choice, we're given our adult names," T'lu-i said.

"And the adult names are awful, stupid names. Like Bear Breath or Flat Nose," Miago added. "My father was called Miago-pi. Now he's called Thunder Fly. Ha!"

"When is this ceremony?"

Miago lowered his voice. "The next full moon." He tapped his forehead. "This is where we'll be marked."

"You call those *marks*? They look like *brands* to me."

Miago heard the man's words but he refused to acknowledge them. For a moment he imagined he was setting snares in the forest, but when that didn't work he was fishing from a canoe. But the Life Choice ceremony was always there, lurking at the back of his mind. He tried to smile at T'lu-i.

"Are you all right?" she asked.

"I think so." He turned to the man. "Last year a girl forgot that we aren't allowed to call it branding." His voice fell to a whisper. "She was overheard. They threw her in prison. Her cell was so crowded that she slept standing up. Now she's too scared to speak in public."

"I see. You said "they" threw her in prison."

"Yes. Our Men of Knowledge."

"The ones in cloaks and hoods?"

"Yes."

The Maker laughed. "It's a good name for them," he finally said. "They certainly have plenty of knowledge."

HIDDEN TREASURE

Miago entered the family shrine. He rang the bell to dispel evil spirits and lit the herb bundle, which soon perfumed the room with smoke. Kneeling, he started his prayers with the words he had recited since childhood: "Banakaloo-Piki, Great Goddess of Fire and Thunder, guide and protect our Men of Knowledge, safeguard my family and hurl disease, starvation and suffering upon the Moroks."

He was facing the black disk bordered with yellow that he knew as the Emblem of Penance. "Great Goddess, thank you for the recent eclipse," he said, as he remembered how the village had stilled and the forest's night soul had woken. The birds had fallen silent and bats filled the sky. "Was it a sign that the Time of Darkness is ending? Is it your wish that the old symbol of the sun is restored? We await your decree from the Men of Knowledge."

Miago rose. He bowed to the statue of Banakaloo-Piki and placed a handful of snuff in the offering cup. "Receive this gift … in return please give me the courage I need to make my Life Choice." A wave of fear washed through him as he struggled to control his racing thoughts. His voice filled with passion, "I beg you, Great Goddess, don't let me flinch or scream when they press the red hot branding iron against my forehead."

With a leap, he was out of the shrine. He leaned on the wall, breathing heavily. "Learn to control yourself, Miago, or you'll never survive," he whispered. He needed to get out of the house, to have space around him. He shouted, "Mother I'm going out to … to look for bamboo …" He didn't wait for her answer. Soon he was filling his lungs with the scented forest air but he stopped before he reached the bamboo thicket. He ducked behind a bush and waited. When he was certain no one was following him, he took the path that led to the volcano. If someone challenged him, his excuse was ready: he needed the strangling vine that grew on its slopes for the new claw-stick's bindings.

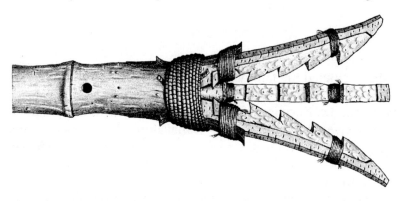

Miago climbed quickly until he came to a bush laden with clusters of golden berries. He popped one in his mouth and smiled as the taste of honey burst on his tongue. Soon his pockets were bulging with them. He remembered his last trip and how his mother had hidden the berries in a chest in the garden. When the others weren't looking, she'd sneak out, returning later a little flushed and a lot better at dealing with his father's tantrums.

Miago maintained a good pace as he climbed. Years of practice had taught him to move quickly and silently in the forest. He wondered at the beauty around him, a beauty that often held danger as he passed a blackened tree trunk, shattered by lightning. He knew that other dark forces stalked the forest and that to show them disrespect invited terrible reprisals: there was the hunter impaled on his spear, the egg collector who crawled back blinded. Miago rounded a bend; before him stood a great slab of granite which had been hewn flat and polished. On it was painted the Emblem of Penance. Its base was encircled with offerings – he saw flowers, animal skins and a tethered coconut crab that waved its claws in outrage. Beyond the rock lay a thick bank of mist. Would it lift? Would ghostly figures appear? But all he saw above the mist was the barren, smoking peak of the volcano, the scattered cloud and the soaring falcons. But behind it, where the vegetation ended and his nightmares began, was the jagged entrance to the caves.

The air was cooler here and Miago thought how pleasant it would be during the hottest part of the day but others shared his fear and it drove them away. As he willed the mist to part, he remembered the rumours about the network of caverns and tunnels that emerged somewhere near the ocean.

Like everyone, Miago had heard the stories of hidden treasure. People said gold bars littered the cave floor. Some talked of scatterings of emeralds and mounds of silver conch shells. Others claimed that if there was treasure, it was neither gems nor gold and that a search for them would end in failure.

He had tried discussing it with his parents. "You'd be a fool to enter the caves in the hope of getting rich. In fact, you'd be a fool to go in there for any reason!" his father had bellowed. The next day Miago had given his mother a handful of honey berries. He'd watched her eat them before his questions started.

"Oh, you know I am not allowed to talk about it!"

"I'll get more berries …" he coaxed.

She had drawn a deep breath. "It's difficult to know what to believe because there are so many stories. Yes, people talk about treasure. Maybe the Befores hid their valuables there. People warn that you can't trust your eyes because the caves play with your mind." She leaned forward and placed her hands on his shoulders. "But everyone agrees on one thing," her voice lowered, "no one gets out alive."

Miago stood on the jetty. He'd begged a ride with one canoe, worked the reef for shells and returned with another. Now his catch was spread out and he was sorting it by size and colour. He reached for a stick and tapped a shell. A needle shot out and scratched the stick, leaving a drop of liquid behind. "To think so pretty a shell … could kill a man," he said. He heard shouting.

Looking up he saw two men facing each other.

They were silhouetted against the light and Miago saw how one towered above the other. It wasn't the only difference; the smaller man was thin whereas the other was barrel-chested and muscular. Miago prepared himself for a bloodbath. The larger man raised his fists and shouted, "Come on, if you dare!" His opponent charged forward, arms flailing as he tried to land a blow, but he connected only with air. He stopped, swore and rushed in to land a punch on the bigger man's shoulder. A kick missed, he swung again but the blow was blocked by a thick, hairy arm.

"You call that fighting?" shouted the bigger man as he swiped his enemy with a backhand and followed with a straight right to the jaw. Miago winced at the crunch of knuckle on skull as the smaller man wobbled drunkenly. He was kicked and thrown down, and his groans reached Miago who watched in frozen fascination. Now they grappled in the sand and the smaller man was pinned face down. His limbs jerking, he thrashed and struggled. Would he be killed? Miago wondered if he should try and help. Perhaps if he shouted something … without getting too close? But other men were approaching. The bigger man was laughing and taunting his victim as they dragged him off. Only one man laughed like that: Monkey Blood. Miago returned to work to a chorus of coughing and swearing.

Later, when Miago looked up again, he saw both men were now sitting. They faced a third man who motioned to Miago to join them. There was something familiar about the tattered clothing, the stick that jutted from the sand.

Miago hesitated but he had nothing better to do so he walked over. Monkey Blood's sullen voice boomed up and down the beach. "Fool! If Brine Shrimp had handled the canoe properly, my net wouldn't be stuck in the reef."

"I won't work with you again, Monkey Blood. I was only trying to help you because your canoe sank."

"If I'd wanted your stinking help, I'd have asked for it."

Miago was close now and he was staring at the third man. Yes, though the grey stubble now had the makings of a beard,

it still matched the grey of the eyes.

"Miago, join us please! We are enjoying a lively conversation," the Maker said warmly.

"Do we have to have a spotty boy here?" Monkey Blood roared and with a belch he stormed off.

The Maker smiled at Miago before he turned to study Brine Shrimp. His eyes now seemed to scan the man in minute detail and Miago could feel Brine Shrimp's discomfort. The Maker finally spoke. "Are you in a hurry to join your ancestors?"

"The fight you mean?"

The Maker nodded. "You're half his size but you let your anger take over. You attacked him head-on."

The fisherman looked confused. "But how do you fight a giant?"

"You control your temper and you think. Never play your opponent's game."

Miago leaned forward to listen. Perhaps he could learn something useful.

"Go on," said Brine Shrimp.

"Why didn't you throw sand in his eyes? Or you could have pretended to kick him in the stomach then punched him on the nose." The Maker swung low at an imaginary target. "Crack! One to the ribs." He repeated the blow, this time higher. "Boom! One to the chin."

Miago punched the air and kicked the sand. "Take that, you big bully! Wham! Had enough, have you?"

"And remember, the blows they don't see coming do the most damage."

The fisherman was impressed. "Where did you learn all this?"

The Maker turned and walked away, leaving the question unanswered. Miago followed him. The Maker spoke when he drew level. "Monkey Blood is so angry. Does he fight a lot?"

"Yes."

"Does he drink?"

Miago laughed. "All day long. Why?"

"Have you ever seen him happy?"

"They say he's only happy when he's fighting a big shark from a small canoe in a rough sea."

"I see." He paused. "I think he has a secret."

"Oh?"

"Anyway, I am pleased we ran into each other because I need some cowries. Do you have any you can spare?"

"I can get them. What are they for?"

"A belt. And can you get me some cone shells?"

Miago had seen the wonderful shell belts that merchants sold in the markets. T'lu-i had talked about selling them but he knew that she would want something a little different. "I caught a cone shell earlier."

"The brown and white ones look best but they're the most dangerous," the Maker warned.

"I can handle them."

The Maker changed the subject. "As you know I have no money but there must be a way of paying."

Miago thought about his family and his friends. He had so many questions, so few answers. "I need someone to talk to. Someone who doesn't think like everyone else around here. What if you paid me with words?"

"Words?"

Miago looked up, his eyes wide.

"What's troubling you, Miago?"

Miago tried to marshal his thoughts. "You arrive here, no one knows where from. You seem different." He paused. "Who are you?"

The Maker smiled warmly. "Who would you like me to be?"

"I don't know." *If my family and friends won't talk to me, maybe he will.* "Will you talk to me?" Miago asked.

"Of course. After sunset, here on the beach? I need to come back for something."

"What?"

"Driftwood. The best pieces are sometimes left by the tide."

"What are you going to make?"

"You'll find out."

"Somehow I know you won't tell me! All right. I'll see you later."

Miago watched the Maker go. The sun had shifted so he moved up the beach to find shade. He settled on the sand and stretched out his body. Eyes closed, he hoped for sleep but at first only thoughts came to him: there was Monkey Blood who seemed determined to have no friends. How could he live that way? Then there was the Maker who had appeared from nowhere and was unlike anyone he knew. Miago remembered what he had said about fighting. *Could he teach me to use a knife?*

Miago woke with a yelp. He slapped his ankle and jumped up. He brushed his legs, cursing as he began to run.

He slowed at a fork in the path, choosing the track that led into the forest. He walked uphill and stopped at a ridge of rock. Looking down at the village he saw the ruined buildings as his imagination took over: he felt the ground shaking as the steaming fissure burst open. They said the crack raced down the slope as trees and buildings, terrified animals and screaming people were swallowed by the enraged goddess. Her fury swept through the city as she showered her victims with smoking rocks. The old ones told how the fissure revealed the goddess's glowing heart and the molten blood that flowed there. A great ledge of rock had slipped beneath the waves, taking much of the city with it. With a roar that stampeded animals even in distant lands, the crack had clamped shut to swallow a civilization.

Miago studied the old palace. Despite its fractured profile, it seemed to radiate a majesty that spread to the surrounding buildings. When his gaze fell on the black temple, he sighed. He saw the pink wash in the evening sky and he thought of the merchants charged with matching that colour in stone, of the wagon trains that delivered it and the masons who fashioned it. He remembered the vision when swimming and he wondered at the world his ancestors had known. He stared at the temple again. "Why would anyone paint a temple black?" he shouted. Liking the idea that no one could hear him, he added, "And why lock it?"

A movement caught Miago's eye and now he was watching a laden cart that thundered along a forest track. The cart disappeared behind a bend but he knew the track ended at the temple. The crack of the driver's whip prompted him to wonder why he was in such a hurry.

Curious, Miago hurried downhill to a new vantage point. In the failing light, he saw that the cart had stopped by the back door of the temple. It had been unloaded. A cloaked figure emerged from the shadows. "Which one of them are you?" Miago hissed. The driver was handed something. Money? He bowed to the cloaked figure and, limping, he climbed back on the cart. Miago cringed at the brutality with which he whipped the mule as he drove back up the track.

Miago kept low. The cart was closer; soon it would pass beneath him. He parted the vegetation as the evening light flashed on the gold jewellery that adorned the driver's neck. The bald head, fat stomach and grotesquely swollen leg confirmed his suspicions: it was T'lu-i's father.

Miago was still thinking about the cart when he returned to the beach. Ahead he could make out a shape sitting by a crackling fire. The Maker was studying a strip of leather on which he'd arranged some shells. Miago smiled in greeting and rubbed his swollen calf.

"I was bitten in my sleep," he said.

"Fire ant?"

"Yes. It still hurts."

"It will for a while. If it hurts tomorrow I will give you something to rub on it. Come closer." The Maker bent forward and examined the swelling. "I don't think it left its jaws in you."

Miago saw how the Maker's features danced in the light of the flames and how his eyes held their own fire. He saw the stubble and the dirty, worn clothes. Perhaps this strange man was once a prosperous merchant from a distant land now well down on his luck. Miago knew that some older people didn't like to be asked questions but he decided to take a risk because this strange man interested him. If no one else would listen to him, perhaps he would.

"Why have you come here?" Miago asked.

"I've come here in search of someone."

"A wife?"

The man laughed. "No."

"Who?"

"I don't know yet."

Miago sighed. The Maker might be prepared to talk, but he didn't seem to be answering Miago's questions and that was almost worse. "At least tell me where you've come from."

"I've come from somewhere close to here, that's very far away."

"You're playing games with me!"

"One day I hope you will understand."

"Understand?" Miago kicked at the sand. "I thought perhaps

you'd help me but this is a waste of time."

"One day I hope all your people will understand."

Miago sat in silence. Perhaps he should leave now. He was about to rise but he tried again. "Tell me about where you've come from."

The Maker smiled; it was as if his mind was elsewhere. "I come from a place of great beauty. There is lush vegetation, golden sand, so much fruit you'd never go hungry. Whatever grows here … well, there it's bigger. Sweeter. And the animals …"

"… the animals?"

"… have no need to fear men."

"So where is this place? Can I go there?"

"No."

"Why not?"

"You aren't ready."

"Why do you talk like this? You know I don't understand you. I'm going home."

"Before you go …"

"What?"

"I too have a question."

Was this strange man playing games? But he seemed kind and intelligent and no one had spoken to Miago like this before. Though his frustration was building, so was his curiosity. "What is it?"

"So tell me, Miago," the Maker said casually, "what does it all mean?"

Miago was surprised by the question. "What does … what mean?"

The Maker used his stick to draw in the sand. "When I arrived, the first thing I noticed was that every adult had a scar on their forehead. The first man I saw had one like this."

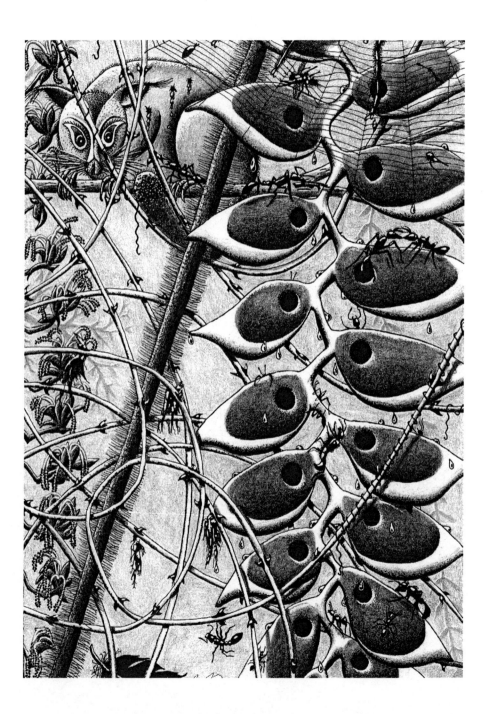

"That mark means he's a Worker," Miago explained.

The Maker raised an eyebrow. "Indeed? Tell me, what is a Worker?"

"Workers live their lives doing physical things. They are our soldiers, fishermen, they repair our houses so they develop their bodies."

"Only their bodies?"

"Yes. Those are the rules."

The Maker considered this. "I see. In the language of the ancients, that person is called a *to*." He shifted in the sand. "So they're the worker ants?"

Miago considered this. "I suppose so but you need two other types of people to make the world work ..."

The Maker raised his hand. "What a grand statement! Where does all this come from?"

"Our Men of Knowledge," said Miago.

"Of course it does! And the other types?"

"We have the Thinkers. They use their brains and teach, record our history, work out better ways of doing things." Miago took the stick and, after a few sweeps, he pointed. "That's their mark."

"They sit with their legs tucked underneath them." Miago struggled to adopt the position before giving up, laughing. "I'm no good at it!"

"It's based on the thin-eyed men who sit this way to still their minds. The ancients called this *ca*."

Miago unwrapped his legs. He'd never heard of thin-eyed people; in fact, so much of this was new to him. "How do you know about this?"

"Because I am well travelled."

Miago leaned forward. "You've seen people who sit like this?"

"Oh, yes," the Maker shrugged, "and many other peoples who, to you, would look and behave strangely."

Miago was confused. "But there are my people and there are the Moroks. My father talks of a few other scattered tribes and groups, but ..."

The Maker smiled. "Miago, there's a world you've never dreamed of." His expression changed. "There's a land where men hunt great hopping beasts that carry their young in a pocket!"

"These monsters wear clothes?"

"And guess what the hunters use for a weapon?"

"A spear? Bow and arrow?" He tried again. "No, they set a trap?"

"They throw a curved stick. It they miss, it comes back."

"By magic?"

"Imagine this beach, Miago. There are lands that are nothing but sand. No trees, no water ... where great animals carry people on their humped backs."

Miago was trying to make sense of this but the Maker was already speaking of other exotic places. "There are men who make snakes dance to music; others who paint their faces blue and build great stone circles to their gods ... some men make houses from blocks of ice and travel on chairs pulled by dogs."

Miago had a dozen more questions and was unsure where to start. "What's ice?" he said but the Maker didn't answer. It was late and Miago knew his father would demand to know where he'd been but he continued. "The last type is the Believers. Their lives are served in the glory and worship of the gods. They are our priests and our healers and they work to appease the Goddess of Fire and Thunder. Their mark looks like this."

The Maker nodded. "Ah, a *mu*. It's named after an advanced, spiritual people. Now tell me, are there more pictures?"

"No. Why?"

The Maker changed the subject. "Monkey Blood didn't have a clear mark. His scar was smudged."

"He struggled. It took six soldiers to hold him down ..."

"Why do they call him Monkey Blood?"

"Because no one knows who his father was." Miago lowered his voice. "They say that includes his mother."

The Maker was silent. "The marking," he said at last, "how long has it been going on for?"

Miago counted on his fingers. "This will be the ninth year. In the first year every adult was marked and the ceremony took many days. This time it will be those born in my year."

"Why did it start?" the Maker pressed.

"It was a new decree from our Men of Knowledge. They said that greater efforts were needed to appease Banakaloo-Piki."

"Greater efforts?" the Maker repeated, frowning.

Miago nodded. "In spite of everything we do – the ceremony, the adult names, painting the temple black, locking it up – still she is angry with us."

"Are there any good rules?"

"Some. Last year they decreed any man could carry a knife to defend himself against the Moroks."

The Maker stood and smoothed away the images in the sand. "Branding, a black temple, knives," he said, almost to himself. He nodded his head at the shadows behind Miago. "And we're being watched. It's better we leave this for now."

Miago turned as the Maker prodded the fire with his stick, producing a burst of flame. It illuminated the beach and a man who was crouching in the shadows. He buried his head in his tunic and hurried away.

"Do you know him?" asked the Maker.

Miago groaned. "Yes, he's a spy. Now I'm in trouble."

"Can I guess who he spies for?"

"The Men of Knowledge."

"Of course."

THEY ONLY TALK
IN WHISPERS

Miago checked the balance of the claw-stick. He pushed the last of the weights into the bamboo cavity and bound the grippers he'd carved from leopard wood. He reinforced them with iron pegs. Good, he thought. It was not only the longest claw-stick he'd made, it was also the best and soon he'd get to use it.

He left his work when his mother shouted that the meal was ready. What mood would his father be in tonight? Miago wondered if he should sit silently, perhaps even agree with his father. Or maybe the time had come to argue back.

Miago squeezed onto the bench beside his sister. His father, a gaunt and restless man, recited the Prayer of Thanks. His mother, round and soft, busied herself while the others ate.

"Smells good," Miago said.

"It's pygmy lobster but I mixed a new spice with it. The merchant said it would bring out the flavour."

Miago's father wiped his sweating forehead. "Silver Rain, why must you make everything so spicy?"

"I'm sorry, dear. I hoped you would like it."

"Well, I don't." Thunder Fly pushed his plate away. "Go and get me something I can eat."

She left the room and Miago heard a sob that she tried to disguise as a cough.

She returned with dried fish and fruit. "It's all I have dear." She said.

They finished the meal in silence. Then Thunder Fly stood and with a nod he dismissed Miago's sister from the room.

"Miago," he began. "Your mother and I need to know if you have made your Life Choice."

He avoided eye contact. "No, Father."

"How difficult can it be?" he shouted. "There are only three choices!"

Miago was silent.

"If you don't, they will choose for you. Do you want that to happen?" Thunder Fly sighed. "I saw your uncle today. He told me Damago has decided."

Miago picked at a fingernail that was already too short. A stab of pain brought a drop of blood but he kept picking.

"Are you listening to me, young man?"

Miago felt a surge of anger that built inside him. His palms were sweating but he was determined to stand his ground. "I'm not like Damago. He's always known his path."

"There's so little time," his father growled. "Do you want to end up like Monkey Blood? The idiot has no friends, he's always fighting ..." His voice rose. "Do you want to be banished to a sand-flat to live with the sea snakes?"

"At least he gets to watch the pelicans," Miago answered quietly.

"Last year he killed a dolphin. What if an ancestor's spirit was in it?" Thunder Fly roared.

"Maybe it was an accident?"

His father was shouting, "You defend that troublemaker?"

"I ..."

"Don't interrupt! He left his net out because he was drunk!"

"Please don't shout at him," Silver Rain interrupted, glancing anxiously at both in turn. "You know it doesn't help. Give him time ..."

Miago thanked his mother with a wink. His father was talking again.

"Time? He has no time! Why isn't my son ... normal?" he added despairingly.

"He is normal. Perhaps a little confused," offered his mother.

"You think seeing things is normal?"

"The visions have stopped, haven't they, Mudskipper?" she asked.

"I wish you wouldn't call me that," Miago said. "I'm not a child."

Miago could feel his father's eyes on him. "Answer your mother, Miago."

"I haven't had a vision in years."

Silver Rain placed her hands on the boy's neck and kneaded it gently. He relaxed as her fingers probed and squeezed. Then she started to work on his shoulders. Her words were soft. "Mudskipper, you know that we only want you to be happy."

Miago saw the contempt in his father's face. He heard it in his words. "Sometimes I wonder whether you think like one of those … what were they called? The ones who all died in the caves."

"They called themselves," he spoke quietly, "the Red Orchids."

"Red Orchids! What sort of name is that?" shouted Thunder Fly. "Stupid name, stupid people! Ten of them went in, none came out! Every year others try. When will they learn?" He banged his fist on the table. "Did they ever think of the dishonour they brought on their families? Who will look after their parents in old age? All these years we prepare you for the ceremony so you can take your place in society. Have I ever asked for anything other than obedience?"

Thunder Fly stopped pacing. "Son, I have spoken to your mother and we think you'd be best suited as a Worker. That way you can continue to collect shells, help in the market, make things to sell … and you'll have the honour of defending us against the heathen marauders. Remember that if you kill ten Moroks our family name will be carved on the Sun Stone in the Great Chamber."

Miago had heard this speech many times. As usual his father was thinking only about himself. Miago spoke under his breath, "The Sun Stone isn't in the Great Chamber. They locked it in the temple because of the cracks in the floor."

"If you have something to say, speak up!"

"It's all about honour and family name and … and killing Moroks, isn't it? Well, you failed there, Father! What makes you think I'd do better?"

"I killed ten of them!" his father bellowed. "But one sneaked off and died in the forest! And you know the rule: no skull, no kill."

"For once, can't you tell me something I haven't heard before?"

There was a strange, dead silence and Miago saw the look that passed between his parents.

"So you want a new story, do you?" Thunder Fly said finally.

Silver Rain buried her face in her hands. "No! Please don't tell him. Not *that*!"

"He's old enough to know, woman!"

There was something in the glance that passed between his parents, a look Miago hadn't seen before and, as his father started speaking, Miago felt a shiver run down his spine.

"It happened one moonless night. Those are the nights when they come among us because ... Moroks can see in the dark."

Miago pictured the crouching, unclothed giants as they sneaked through the village. There was grunting and the buzz of flies. He imagined the wiry hair that coated their sinewy bodies as they bounded ditches and scaled walls. Hunched, they ran silently past the sleeping dogs; from roof to roof they crawled to peer through windows in search of unguarded children.

"Can they really see in the dark?"

"Yes. And they came to this house." Thunder Fly drew a deep breath. "Son, I had worked hard that day, I was watching for them at the window, axe in hand but it was warm and quiet ... I fell asleep. When I woke, he was gone."

Miago's mouth had gone dry. He felt dizzy as he forced out the question, dreading the answer. "Who was gone?"

"Cufu," his father whispered.

He stared at his parents in turn. "But you, you said he died from rain fever?"

Thunder Fly turned away.

Silver Rain wiped her eyes. "It's true he'd been ill but he was getting stronger. All we know is that he disappeared in the night. They sent a patrol out at first light but the Moroks had broken camp. Your father followed them for days but they were too fast."

Miago's voice was strangled. "Poor Cufu. If I ever see a Morok ..."

There was desperation in Silver Rain's voice. "Did they eat

him? Did they shackle him in chains and work him to death?"

"And ..." his father added brokenly, "I'm to blame." He grabbed Miago's wrist and held it tightly. "As a Worker you will have the chance for vengeance. Remember that!"

New feelings swept through Miago. "But what about what *I* want, what about what would make *me* happy? What –"

Thunder Fly interrupted. "Trust me when I say we're lucky to have Men of Knowledge. The Befores perished because their ways were wrong. Be thankful our laws will soon prevent you asking questions and making the same mistakes as them. Look at the misery of the plains nomads or the battles that rage between the river tribes ... think of the wars between the Dog People and the forest pygmies. As for the Moroks! Why are their lives nothing but war, illness and suffering? Because they have no guidance. You should be grateful for who you are. Without our Men of Knowledge we'd be no better than them." He spat on the floor.

There was a knock and Miago's sister entered. "What are you talking about?"

"Moroks," Miago answered.

She giggled. "Oh? Why do they have big ears?"

Miago sighed. "I'm bored of your jokes, Rain Dancer."

"Because they only talk in whispers."

"Very funny," Miago said.

"How do you track a Morok in the dark?"

"You follow the flies," Miago replied automatically. He turned to his parents. "If I become a Worker, I'll never be allowed to use my mind. And what about T'lu-i? What if she decides to be a Thinker? Then we'll never be together."

"T'lu-i is a lovely girl and you're well suited," his mother said, relieved at the change of subject.

Thunder Fly drew himself to his full height. "Son, one day you'll thank me. Now go to the shrine and pray."

"That's another thing." Miago paused. "Why must I worship a black circle?" He stood defiantly to face his father. He saw the veneer of strength, the man's stubborn armour, but was there something new in the tone of his voice? Miago probed deeper. "Why haven't they brought back the old symbol of the sun?

We have just had an eclipse. What clearer sign could you ask for? We all expected a decree but none came! Why, Father? Why?"

Miago saw how he turned to Silver Rain for support. How she looked away. "Miago, I heard that the Men of Knowledge spoke with Banakaloo-Piki after the eclipse," he said uncertainly. "Perhaps she told them the time wasn't right. Or maybe they will make an announcement at the ceremony."

The women nodded. "Yes, that must be it," his mother said. "The Sun Symbol will be restored at the ceremony."

"It's obvious!" his sister added.

But Miago had more questions. "Our Men of Knowledge ..."

"What is it now, son?"

"Why do they dress like that?"

"Like what?"

"In those hooded cloaks?"

"You know it's their custom," Thunder Fly said. "Don't read anything into it."

"Then why do people say you'll go mad if you see their faces?"

Silver Rain put her hand on his arm. He felt the warmth. "Mudskipper, if I believed everything I heard around here ..."

"And that they may sound like people but they can take any form they want."

"Oh Miago ..."

It seemed so pointless arguing because he knew none of them would change. "I'm going to bed." He kissed his mother and sister. He hesitated before offering his hand to his father. It was ignored.

Thunder Fly's face hardened. "I have a final question. And I demand the truth."

Miago's hand dropped as his fear rose. *Be very careful.* "What, Father?"

"You were seen talking to a stranger in the market. Who was he?"

"Oh, him?" Miago tried to sound relaxed. "He only wanted a conch."

"You were also seen with him on the beach, young man."

Miago was silent but he felt his father's untrusting eyes

burning into him. He stepped back, closer to the door, closer to freedom.

"Talking to strangers is dangerous. You aren't to see him again. Understand?" Thunder Fly said.

Why hadn't he pursued the question? He must have known I had no answer ... Miago spoke carefully, "Yes, Father." As he left the room, he was still thinking about it. Was his father tired? Or perhaps he wasn't quite so sure of himself as he pretended.

Miago sat on the edge of his bed and glanced around the room. Thoughts tumbled in on him, as they always did when he was alone. He pictured the Palace of Peace where the Men of Knowledge lived and the humble, broken homes of the villagers. He thought of the busy market and of the merchants who complained about the taxes they paid, of the cracked streets and invasive forest.

When Miago thought of the Moroks, he grew angry. They would soon return to the plains beyond the forest with their mangy cattle, their filthy women and black tents. The howls of their dogs would carry on the breeze, the stench of their camp would bring flies and drive the wild animals away. Which children would they take this time?

T'lu-i came to him and there was excitement mixed with a dreamy stillness. Cufu entered his thoughts too and Miago was smiling at the mischief in his brother's eyes. He relived a fishing trip, and he heard again Cufu's shriek when the blowfish they caught swelled in anger. There were swimming lessons, one that ended with them coughing and spluttering in the surf after they'd been bowled over by a wave. Miago pictured the soldier crabs they chased at low tide, the crocodiles they tormented with stones ... and always there was laughter.

Miago saw Cufu sleeping. He imagined the contorted shape that squeezed between the window bars. His nose twitched

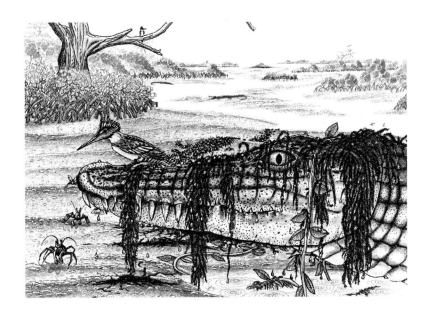

at the bitter smell. He writhed as the crouching Morok emerged from the shadows. Was Cufu drugged in his sleep and carried off in the man's shoulder bag? One hand pulled the pillow over his head, the other punched the wall. "Why, Cufu, why did they take *you*?" he sobbed.

The sounds of his distress carried to his parents' room.

"I must go to him," Silver Rain cried.

"No," Thunder Fly commanded. "The time has come to leave him."

"But he needs me!"

"Obey me, woman!"

She turned her back on her husband and spoke calmly. "You push him too hard and you know what? It won't work with him."

HE COLLECTS
DEAD THINGS

Miago didn't see the Maker the next day. To keep his mind off the ceremony he joined his cousin Hard Hands to help a group of men clear a section of forest.

The leader walked the plot before marking its border with stones. Miago watched as he checked the wind direction and studied the plants. He struck a bush with his stick. "Watch out all of you," he warned. "This is puncture vine. Burn it. Then dig up the roots."

Miago carried his father's machete and he was anxious to use it.

"That's a man-sized knife!" someone laughed.

"Make sure you don't cut your arm off!" came a dry response from a man whose naked torso and right arm bulged with muscle, though the other arm hung limp and withered.

"Aren't you worried about the mosquitoes, Fiddler Crab?" Miago asked.

"I've rubbed munjo juice on my skin. You should try it."

Miago wrinkled his nose. "I think I'd rather be bitten."

They started by clearing a border around the plot. Soon Miago was bathed in sweat but he enjoyed the hacking and cutting as the stubborn roots became his enemies. A blow would sever an arm, a second would bring a whoop of delight. "Die, Morok!" There was moisture in the plants and he helped soak the plot in whale oil to get a fire started. When it caught, the flames worked with the wind, consuming everything in a blazing frenzy. They stood back from the searing heat and crackling plants and Miago watched as the twisting plumes of smoke carried the ash away. Fiddler Crab dropped his knife and began to sing, "Oh the life of a Worker me, I'd rather a Thinker be, but rules is rules is rules, and I can't outsmart a tree ..."

"You sing as badly as Miago!" shouted Hard Hands.

Miago felt the warmth that told him he was blushing. *Thanks for telling everyone, Hard Hands.* He scratched at the soil with his sandal. "Look at that!" he said, turning to his cousin. "It's redder than in the village."

Hard Hands pulled up a blackened root, his face straining with effort. "You know the story about why it's red?"

Miago frowned. "Which one?"

"The one about the wise man they murdered in the forest. The soil's red with his blood."

Miago nodded. "They say happiness will only return when all his blood's washed out to sea." He thought of the red soil that ran high into the forest, of how it lay beneath the blown sand in the village. He sighed. "That could take ... forever."

In the heat it was better to conserve their strength so the singing and talking stopped. Miago relaxed into a steady rhythm as he hacked and dug. He jumped when someone shouted, "Forest demon!"

The men formed a circle above it. They stared at the long, segmented body.

"Fifty legs each side!"

"You don't want to be bitten by that!"

"It's as long as my arm!"

"Which end is the head?"

The creature flowed over the ground, circling and twisting as it sought to escape. Fiddler Crab jumped in front of it and flipped it over with his machete. He scooped it up and threw it onto some glowing embers and steam burst from its writhing body. He licked his lips. "Maybe I'll eat him on the way home."

They finished the plot at dusk. Walking slowly back, Miago and Hard Hands fell into conversation. "Miago, I've heard most of your year has chosen. Have you?"

Miago winced. *Do you have to bring this up now?* "Not yet."

"Why not?"

Should he answer? Try to change the subject? "Would you like to help me set some snares tomorrow?"

"Miago, we need to talk about this. It's important."

"I haven't chosen because I don't know what T'lu-i will

choose. Part of me wants to be a Worker. Look at Six Toes. I'd like to do as little work as him and have a house that size."

"He's rich because of his fishing potion."

"I know. Do you know what's in it?"

"There are rumours he collects dead things at night. Some say he boils up forest mushrooms with rotting fruit." He paused. "But you have more important things to worry about now."

"Was it difficult for you?"

"No. There wasn't really a choice because I'm built like a buffalo and it would be a waste not to work this magnificent body!" They both laughed. "By making your Life Choice, it means you can get on with your life and leave problems to others."

In a strange way this almost made sense. "So it works for you?"

Hard Hands sounded surprised. "Of course! And there's the chance of glory too." He patted the knife that hung from his belt.

Miago saw the leather sheath that followed the curve of the long blade. A flash of light was playing on the handle. "You got your first Morok last year, didn't you?" he asked.

"Yes. They were coming to poison our water but we surprised them. Four of them, twenty of us. They never stood a chance. One ran off and I tracked him. It took all day but I caught him in Vulture Pass."

"I've never been that far into the forest," Miago said wistfully, as he thought of its further reaches. Few of his friends had; fewer still would talk about it. He imagined how the tracks ended at impenetrable jungle, he saw gnarled, ancient trees and a canopy so thick that it blocked out the sunlight.

"Nor had I until then. It's a beautiful place of cliffs and waterfalls except for the vultures that glide back and forth searching for death. I found the Morok skulking in some bushes. He screamed when he saw me, begged me to spare his life. He even tried to make me pity him by saying he had a sick wife and eight children to feed!"

Miago shared his cousin's excitement. "How did you do it?"

"I told him he was my sworn enemy and that by fathering all those children he was guilty of making more murdering, heathen Moroks. But I said he could go if he swore never to return. He cried

with gratitude and kissed my feet! He was singing with joy as he turned away." Hard Hands chuckled. "I grabbed his hair, pulled his head back and slit his throat! I kept his skull ... left his body for the birds."

Miago imagined the scene. "How did it make you feel?"

"Like a man."

"Wait, you spoke to a Morok?"

Hard Hands nodded, his eyes still dreamy with the memory of his first kill.

"But you don't speak their language."

"Speak their language?" Hard Hands guffawed. "Of course not, if the grunts they make could be called a language!" They both laughed. "I know it's strange but he spoke some of ours."

"He did?" Miago asked in surprise.

Hard Hands started rolling his eyes and grunting. He let a line of spit run down his chin. Miago laughed and tucked his hands into his armpits. He started squatting and shrieking. Hard Hands copied him.

After a minute, Hard Hands waved in surrender. "Miago, I can't! I'm too tired to be a Morok!"

"So am I!" said Miago straightening up. "What about the marking? Did it hurt?" Miago saw the flash of pain in Hard Hands' eyes, how his fingers stroked the scar.

"The important thing is not to show it. Remember – if you are brave it means you've made the right Life Choice."

"I know," Miago said. "But I'm scared and I'm worried I'll show it."

"You must be brave, Miago. Or you will always regret it."

"What about the night before the ceremony when they make you sleep alone in the jungle. What was that like?"

"Terrifying," Hard Hands confessed. "All your life you are warned of the demons that stalk the forest at night, the dead that climb from the volcano ... the evil spirits that enter the bodies of animals to hunt human flesh."

Miago shivered. "What about the palm trees?"

"The ones that lean out over the ocean?"

Miago saw the hanging fronds that tapped the wave tops

like great legs; the cluster of coconuts that formed the hairy body. "Yes. They say they turn into giant spiders that walk on the water in search of sleeping dolphins. Did you sleep near the volcano?"

"I stayed down low. You should too."

"I'm no hero. I will." He looked around. "Over there looks safe but ..."

"What?"

His voice trembled. "What about the Jungle Prowlers?"

Hard Hands gripped Miago's shoulder. "Pray you never meet one of *those*!"

"Some people say they're sent by the Goddess to find anyone who hasn't made their Life Choice."

"Which was why I made mine," Hard Hands said firmly. "Miago, you must too. And soon. Another thing: find a place where you can sleep with your back to the vegetation. The thicker the better."

"Why?"

"So nothing can attack you from behind."

"But I'll be trapped! Nowhere to run if I'm attacked from the front!"

"It's what I did and I survived. Remember Pokilu slept in the open and he disappeared. And his mother gave him flower dust to keep him alert."

Miago hesitated. He remembered Pokilu as a quiet boy; a loner who never broke the rules, who kept his thoughts to himself. "Maybe he planned it ... maybe he ran away?"

"To spend the rest of his life running? If the Men of Knowledge suspected it, they'd have sent Trackers."

Miago's thoughts drifted and he was alone in the moonlit forest. He heard the crack of a twig, the deep growl of an unseen creature. He imagined being watched, circled by a sinewy mass that dragged its belly, whose malevolence was more dark energy than shape. Was it better to drink a sleeping draught and take your chances? Or maybe he should stay awake all night? "Does flower dust keep you awake?" Miago asked.

"You've never tried it?"

Miago shook his head.

"Yes. I'll show you how much to take so that it doesn't eat your brain but you must promise you'll never use it again because each time you use it you'll need more. Soon you can't get enough."

"Can you get me some?"

"Perhaps. And another thing. After the ceremony it's important your scar heals. If you get sick, if the burn fills with banana juice, that's a sign you made the wrong choice and that you'll be a troublemaker. Be sure this doesn't happen. Protect yourself."

"How?"

"You must spend more time in your shrine. Every day make fresh offerings and burn more herbs. And ..." Hard Hands paused.

"Yes?"

"Don't just kneel, throw yourself on the ground before the Emblem. Remember the Great Goddess listens *and* she watches."

A BARRACUDA'S EYE

The ocean was whipped by squalls so Miago couldn't dive. Instead, he went down to the beach and helped drag the canoes ashore. Then he walked along the jetty. A dozen fish traps were balanced there but, unlike the clean traps that lay in neat rows on the beach, these were a mess of split, weed-covered bamboo. A stiff breeze threatened to blow them into the surf. Miago poked one with his foot and a cloud of flies burst from a rotting fish head. There were dozens of fishermen but Miago knew which one refused to respect the spirits of the ocean.

"You really should look after these, Monkey Blood, if you don't want to lose them," he said. An angry voice made him turn.

"Damn him! That idiot's been warned not to leave his stinking traps here. Let's throw them into the sea and teach him a lesson."

There were two men. The taller one's stride was jerky, one shoulder was held higher than the other, an effect that was emphasized by the tilt of the neck. Miago glanced at the deformed foot. *Your fishing potion may make you rich, but your money can't fix your foot.* "Hello, Six Toes," Miago said.

The man nodded. "Do you know Full Wit?" he asked. Before Miago could answer, Six Toes was advancing towards the fish traps. "He's been warned about this ..."

"Don't throw them in. I was about to move them," Miago said, blocking his way.

"Why are you helping *him*?" Six Toes asked in surprise.

Miago lifted a trap.

"Hurry, boy. And dump them by the trees so we don't trip over them," added Full Wit.

Six Toes pinched his nose. "Or smell them! When you've finished, come and help us test Full Wit's latest brilliant idea."

Miago had noticed the plank Full Wit carried. Now he saw

more. "Why have you painted the Emblem on a piece of wood?"

Full Wit was deep in thought. "You could call it … fishing with fear."

Miago struggled past with the trap. "What's that?"

Six Toes laughed. "He'll explain later."

The traps were heavier than Miago expected. When he'd finished, he saw Six Toes standing in the shallows. Full Wit was shouting instructions from the beach.

"How do you fish with fear?" Miago asked on rejoining them.

Six Toes was scratching his head. "You'd better explain, Full Wit."

"The surf fish think the Emblem is a barracuda's eye. If they think they're being hunted, they hide in the bubbles where the water is shallowest."

"But all you've painted is the eye!"

Miago saw smug satisfaction in Full Wit's smile. "That's the brilliant part – it's all you need. The barracuda's stripes fade when it hunts, so it's almost invisible. The surf fish can only see its black eye but they know what it is. So we anchor this off the beach and they will be too scared to swim away."

Miago saw the glare that bounced off the water. "But you can also track a barracuda by its shadow. They can't hide *that*."

"You can?" asked Six Toes. "I didn't know that."

"Nor do the surf fish," added Full Wit.

"Won't you need a net?" Miago asked.

"No, I have another brilliant idea! You and Six Toes must build a ring of stones at the low tide mark. As the water drops, it will trap the fish."

He might be smug but he's clever. "I see why you're a Thinker."

Full Wit pointed at the water. "Put the eye there and secure it with stones," he instructed Six Toes. "Put more stones in front of it." As he made himself comfortable on the sand, he added, "Then all we do is wait."

Six Toes sighed. "It won't work."

"You know what? I know when I'm right about something." Full Wit studied Miago closely. "If I'm wrong, I'll tell you how to make the fishing potion."

"Are you mad? That must be kept secret!" Six Toes shouted.

But Miago was smiling because in his mind he was already counting the money.

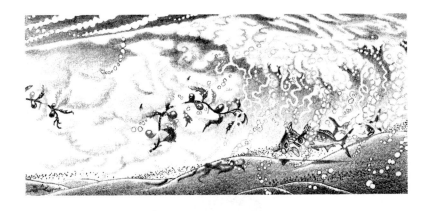

63

Miago was walking through the lower forest. The humidity clung to him like a damp tunic. As there was no market that day, he wondered whether T'lu-i was tending her vegetable patch or collecting windfall fruit. There was movement ahead as a man emerged from the mist. Closer now, Miago recognized him as a friend of Hard Hands. He carried the body of a forest piglet in one hand and a dead macaw in the other, which he raised in greeting.

"Hello, Long Spear. Why are some of its feathers missing?"

"A stranger took them. He had no money but he said he would make me some arrows."

Something sounded familiar. "What did he look like?"

"Let me see. Old clothes, grey beard, thin, softly spoken ..."

"And he carried a stick?"

"You know him?

"We've met."

"I see the fishing was good today, Miago. Are those surf fish?"

Miago shifted the vine that draped from his shoulder to show his catch. "Yes."

"Those aren't easy to catch. Did you use poison?"

"No. We were trying out a new way of fishing."

"Can you spare one?"

Miago slid a fish off the vine. "You can have more."

Long Spear grinned. "One is fine." He patted the piglet. "I finally catch one of these but my wife prefers fish. Women!"

"Which way did the man go?" Miago asked.

Long Spear pointed. "Are you going to follow him?"

Miago nodded and was already striding away. He'd gone some distance when Long Spear shouted, "Be careful, Miago. Talking to strangers can be dangerous!"

"I wish people would stop telling me that," Miago said under his breath. He followed the track deep into the forest.

The sunlight stabbed through the canopy to light the forest floor in a patchwork of dazzling blotches. He heard the drone of insects and the distant screech of a baboon. When he spotted the Maker, he shouted a greeting and jogged ahead.

"Miago, it's good to see you!"

"Hello."

"What can I do for you?"

"Oh, I'm killing time."

"We can't stand here talking." The Maker swatted his arm. "We'll be eaten alive."

"There's a clearing beyond those trees," Miago suggested. "The mosquitoes don't like sunlight and the wind will blow them away."

They sat opposite each other. The Maker was inspecting the macaw feathers that flashed blue and gold. "In some societies these are worn by the elite – the rulers, the priests," the Maker explained. "Now I'm sure I can do something interesting with them …" He looked up. "What is it Miago?"

"People are forever telling me that talking to strangers is dangerous."

The Maker smiled and Miago saw the calmness in his eyes. "Not talking can be more dangerous!"

"You're so … different!"

Now the eyes were laughing. "I hope so!"

Miago was thinking of Full Wit and Six Toes. Suddenly he felt desperate. "What do you do if you work your body *and* use your brain? How can you choose between them? And what if you love a girl who might choose a different mark from you?"

The Maker spoke slowly. "What happens if you don't make a choice?"

"They make it for you," he answered dully.

"Is there an alternative?"

Miago recoiled. "Yes, but it means certain death."

"Oh?"

"First you climb the volcano and then you must earn the right to enter the caves by defeating a Guardian. There are three of them but they aren't ordinary men." He paused. "They're half human, half demon. They guard the entrance to the caves for the Goddess of the Volcano."

"Why are there three of them?"

"One guards what the Thinkers believe, the second protects the beliefs of the Workers, the third's there for the Believers. You must overcome just one of them to enter the caves."

"Why only one?"

"I don't know," said Miago helplessly. "Perhaps they don't make it too difficult so that they can get you inside the caves."

"Why would they want to get you inside the caves?"

Irritation joined Miago's fear. *Does this man know nothing?* "Because they know you'll be killed in there."

"You speak as if it's a certainty, Miago."

He sighed. "No one who's gone in has been seen again."

"Interesting. What happens if you fail to defeat a Guardian?"

"Interesting?" What does he mean by that? "You, you must kill yourself by jumping into the volcano … or you can do it by eating forest mushrooms."

The Maker raised his hand. "I see. Let's suppose you get into the caves. What happens then?"

"You must find your way out." Miago shook his head slowly. "But it's impossible!" he moaned. "There are too many traps."

"What sort of traps?"

"I don't know. But they say the caves are filled with rats and snakes. And ..."

"Yes?"

"Beetles." Miago recoiled. "Huge poisonous, filthy, smelly, brown beetles."

"So you don't like beetles?"

"Does anyone?"

"Do these caves have a name?"

"They call them the Caves of Blindness."

The Maker didn't speak but something else was playing on Miago's mind. "When we spoke about the markings, you had names for them."

"Yes. *To, ca* and *mu.*"

"You seem to know a lot. Do you know how to survive in the caves?"

Instead of answering, the Maker was inspecting the feathers once again.

"You must tell me!"

But he was silent.

"You *must* tell me! Why won't you tell me?"

"You remember when we met?"

"Yes."

The Maker wasn't smiling now. "I told you that I taught people to ask questions. I don't feed them answers."

"But if you know, you must tell me!"

"It wouldn't help if I did."

"I don't understand!"

"Miago, I hope in time that you will. Not just you but your people too. To truly understand, you cannot be told a truth. You must *discover* it for yourself. Anyway, you wouldn't believe me if I told you."

"Why wouldn't I?"

"People never do."

Miago's thoughts were racing. There was the warning not to speak to strangers ... and now Miago was more confused than ever. He felt angry; part of him even wanted to hate this man who wouldn't answer his questions. But the kindness was still shining from the Maker's eyes.

"Who taught *you*?" Miago finally asked.

"My father."

"Is he still alive?"

"Yes."

Miago studied the Maker and added twenty, thirty years. In his mind he whitened his hair and replaced the stubble with a flowing white beard. "He must be very old. I'm sorry. I didn't mean to be rude."

The Maker slapped his thigh and the kind face seemed to open as his smile turned into a deep belly laugh.

SOMEONE TO HATE

Miago combed the village pretending he was running errands as he searched for T'lu-i. He tried to look busy, carrying his sack of shells though he knew few were worth selling. When it came, the booming voice startled him.

"Boy!"

Miago looked up but immediately wished he hadn't.

Monkey Blood was eating peanuts and the crushed nuts and yellow teeth made a revolting combination. Miago hurried on.

"Stop! I want to talk to you."

He was searching for an excuse. "I have to deliver these shells."

Monkey Blood's tone softened. "I wanted to thank you, Miago."

Miago slowed. "Your fish traps? It was nothing."

"You didn't have to do it. If I'd lost them, well, it would have served me right."

Surprised by Monkey Blood's attitude, Miago stopped. "I couldn't let them throw them away."

"No one else would have cared." Monkey Blood was fumbling for something in his tunic. "Peanut?"

"No, thanks."

He found what he was looking for. "This is for you."

The first thing Miago noticed was the blade, shiny and dark, notched near the tip. The metal was decorated with interwoven spirals that swept back to a series of points. He took the knife, his fingers curling around the handle.

Monkey Blood was speaking again. "I've had it for years but it's too small for me. Boy's knife."

Miago tightened his grip as a flash of sunlight lit the blade. "I've never seen one like it. It looks strong." He noticed something. "What are these scratches? They look like crosses."

"Forget them," Monkey Blood said impatiently.

"The blade is very strong and easy to clean."

"Can I use it in the ocean?"

"Look at the colour of the metal. Its maker knew what he was doing. It won't rust. Just wipe it down and it will outlast you … and your children."

"Where does it come from?"

"My father left it for me." Monkey Blood spat on the ground. "Only thing he did leave me apart from trouble."

Miago wanted the knife but he hesitated. "I can't take it if it's from your father."

"Of course you can! I never knew him and it needs a new home."

Miago thought of the fish he could clean with it, the rock oysters it would help him collect.

Monkey Blood read his thoughts. "It will help you work and ... and you could kill anything with it. Even a Jungle Prowler!" He roared with laughter.

Miago stepped back and his mouth fell open. "Have you seen one?"

"Why do you ask?"

Miago's mouth felt dry. He was alone in the moonlit forest ... *Control your thoughts, you fool!* "They say if you don't make your Life Choice, they find you." Monkey Blood was silent, so Miago tried again. "Have you seen one?"

Monkey Blood's voice trembled as sweat beaded his forehead. "Be careful what you eat in the forest."

"The only things I've eaten are honey berries."

"Stick to those."

Miago looked at the knife again. "Thank you. I'll look after it." Monkey Blood was silent so he added, "I'll sleep with it under my pillow in case of Moroks."

"Are you a restless sleeper?"

"Why?"

"I wouldn't want it to cut your ear off!" Monkey Blood laughed and showered Miago's face with chewed peanuts. "Is there something else?"

Miago wiped his face, waiting for an apology that didn't come. He did have more questions but he was wary of Monkey Blood's temper. He started slowly. "They say you killed a dolphin and other bad things about you but you're giving me this knife ..."

"You're a brave one, aren't you? Listen. This place has its laws, just like any place. Most people live by them, I don't." He leaned forward and whispered, "No one has the guts to stand up for what they believe in around here ..."

Miago thought of his father, his family and friends. With surprise he found himself agreeing with Monkey Blood. "Go on."

"So I forgot to check my net. A dolphin got stuck in it and everyone blamed poor old Monkey Blood. You know what?"

"What?"

He grinned. "They should pay me!"

"Why?"

"Because people need someone to hate and I'm happy to oblige. So I leave my nets out, make a mess of the beach ..."

"Were you sad it died?"

"What no one bothered to find out was it was old. No teeth. So how could it catch fish? Maybe my net did that poor dolphin a favour." He clamped his huge hand on Miago's shoulder. "I've things to do."

But Miago wasn't finished. "People say our ancestors' spirits live in dolphins."

The man shrugged. "They say many things."

Monkey Blood didn't seem to be getting angry and Miago was surprised that his answers made sense. So he risked another question. "Have you heard of the Red Orchids?"

But this time Monkey Blood's face tightened and he growled. "What do you know about *them*?"

"They were a group of people who went in the caves."

"Why are you asking *me*?"

"No one will talk about them but they interest me."

Monkey Blood's eyes narrowed as he studied Miago. "You think people who form a blood pact and throw their lives away are ... interesting?"

"A blood pact?"

Monkey Blood sneered. "They cut themselves. Mixed their blood in a shell and drank it. Swore they'd stick together until death."

"And they all died?"

"Every one of them."

"How?"

"Maybe they went swimming where they shouldn't have. How should I know?"

"They say there were ten of them."

Monkey Blood snorted. "It was a long time ago, but there were eleven. One was too scared to go into the caves." He spat on the ground again.

"What happened to him?"

"That coward? Died years ago. Forget it." With a grunt Monkey Blood was gone.

Miago stood there thinking. He raised the knife, marvelling at its design and balance. It felt so good in his hand that it might have been made for him. He slipped it inside his tunic. His thoughts were interrupted by the notes of a song that drifted towards him from the market. He listened carefully. Yes, it was *her* voice. He imagined T'lu-i absorbed in her work, pretending to be unaware of the admiring glances she attracted. He laughed and tried humming along but he soon gave up. He turned a corner and saw her, surrounded by palm leaves and timber poles. A series of holes had been gouged in the ground, reed matting covered the floor. She sat with her legs tucked under her like a Thinker.

She looked up. "Miago! Pass me that ball of twine, will you?"

He hesitated. "Why are you sitting like that?"

T'lu-i stretched her back. Her words came lazily. "Oh, to see what it feels like." She lowered her head to study him through long, curled eyelashes.

Miago tried to look calm. Was she trying to tell him something? He wiped his forehead with the back of his hand. "It's hot today."

She yawned. "Is it?"

Miago was thinking how little time was left. His thoughts raced when he realized he'd been standing there, staring. He searched for something to say. "Can I sell my shells here?"

T'lu-i unravelled a length of twine. "You won't need a stall this big."

"Well," Miago hesitated, "I'm thinking of selling knives too." He showed her the knife. "Like this."

In silence T'lu-i measured a palm.

"You know, the stall would be better with bamboo supports. I know where the best ones grow." Miago offered her the knife. "Try this."

"No, thanks," she replied, glancing at it with distaste. "I'll use my shell cutter."

Miago felt foolish as he slipped the knife back into his tunic. He searched for something to say but she hadn't finished.

"I won't let you sell knives here."

"Why not? Everyone's buying them. You can find good ones if you know the right people."

"I don't care," said T'lu-i coldly. "I hate knives. All you do with them is kill. And the poor trees."

"Trees?"

"Why do people cut their names in them? You can sell your coral and shells here but no knives."

"But I want to make money. Will you ask your father?"

"You can ask him yourself. He's coming to see if this stall is big enough."

"Big enough for what?"

"I don't know but it's something important."

Miago remembered seeing her father deliver a cargo to the temple.

T'lu-i glanced around. "Can you keep a secret?"

He nodded.

"He calls it *black gold.*"

"Oh?"

T'lu-i shrugged. "He won't say what it is but he's sure he's going to get even richer." She smiled. "They don't call him Market Man for nothing."

Her next question caught Miago off guard. "If you want to sell knives, does that mean you're going to be a Worker?" Before Miago could answer she sprang up. "Daddy! Miago wants to rent part of the new stall."

Miago saw Market Man's shifty eyes. His fat, hairless face finished at a double chin, below which flashed a thick gold chain. There was more gold on his stubby fingers. Miago knew not to stare at the blackened, swollen leg. The man was smiling. I'd smile too, Miago thought, if I was as rich as you. "Hello, Market Man, sir," he said, regretting his next words even as he spoke them, "I saw you the other night."

The shifty eyes narrowed. "Where?"

He thought quickly. "Leaving the … market. I was going to ask your advice about the secret to trading."

Market Man studied him carefully. "Rule one: trust no one," he said sharply. "Rule two: trust no one. Can you guess rule three?"

Miago nodded. "I think so, sir."

T'lu-i interrupted. "If we rent him space he can't sell knives."

"No knives?" Market Man asked, raising his eyebrows. "Why not?"

T'lu-i put her arms round her father and hugged him. Miago could see the outline of her body through her thin dress. He tried not to stare as she smiled at her grinning father.

"All right. If you don't want him to sell knives, then no knives it is! That's a promise!" He slapped his daughter playfully on the bottom and said, "Has your father kept you happy? Has he done his best for his special girl?"

"Oh yes, Daddy!"

Market Man patted her head. "The only girl to run her own stall and she does it as well as anyone!" He smiled at Miago. "Way to a woman's heart? Give her what she wants!"

"You make me so happy, Daddy."

Market Man was grinning even more broadly. "Well, we have to look after each other now it's only the two of us."

Miago had had enough. He said something about mending a net and left, hurrying away until he reached a line of palms, where he stopped. Leaning against a tree he saw the scratched writing and the loving messages. He took out the knife and carved T'lu-i's name in the bark. He was about to add his own, but was there any point, he wondered. Miago walked on until he came to the beach. He boarded a canoe and paddled across the lagoon to a line of tidal nets. He anchored and climbed a lookout pole. Then he reached into his pocket and drew out a handful of crumbs which he threw into the water. Soon it was boiling with the silver flashes of feeding fish. From his other pocket he took a small package. He unwrapped it and sprinkled its contents over the fish. He watched as they carried on feeding. When they darted away he laughed. "Well, that isn't Six Toes' potion!"

The fish were gone and he was staring at the setting sun. Should he ignore his concerns and choose the same mark as T'lu-i? What if that led to a lifetime of suffering? If only he could win her and avoid being marked but that meant taking the cave challenge. He pictured the blackness of the caves and his mind raced from giant snakes to rats and vampire bats. He saw broken bones and crushed skulls. But it was the image of a giant beetle, with its horned head, hooked feet and armoured body that made him shudder.

He spoke aloud. "Don't be so stupid, Miago. You wouldn't even get past the Guardians."

STRIPED DEATH

Miago crouched in the prow of a canoe, the warmth of the sun on his back. A broad-shouldered man, his thick forearms a mass of entwined tattoos, pulled smoothly on a paddle. Despite his bulk, Miago admired the precision with which he controlled their drift. A third man jigged a feather lure in their wake but Miago saw the boredom in his work. "Looks like we'll go hungry tonight," the man complained. The water here was clear and the current wasn't too strong. Miago followed the darkening ocean towards a bank of mist and cloud. A voice interrupted his thoughts.

"Don't even think of swimming to Offal Rock … unless you want to be eaten by cockroaches." The man was coiling his fishing line.

"I was checking the current because I don't want to be swept anywhere near that island, Rock Cod."

The other man joined in. "Look at the current mid-channel. I'm not paddling against that to rescue you."

Miago glanced at the gourd by the man's legs. "A different mixture, Painted Arms?"

"Yes. Don't swim in it – it might burn your skin."

"You won't get a good price for your fish if they look damaged."

"Let's see if it works first. I'll wait until you are a long way away."

Miago raised his claw-stick. He patted the new knife that was sheathed at his waist before checking his goggles; he kneaded the gum that secured the turtle-shell lenses. "I'll dive here and meet you at the end of the reef. You'd better have another sack ready for me!"

Painted Arms glanced over his shoulder then back at the boy. "Watch out for jellyfish. That turtle we saw can't eat them all."

Miago pulled a fishing lure from his bag. "You should try this, Rock Cod. Work it against the current so it chugs along. If it catches fish I'll make more to sell in the market. Tell me if the hook rusts." He balanced on the side of the dugout and slipped into the water between the hull and outrigger. He felt how the water had been chilled by the wind and he saw that it was unusually clear. Below him were the undulations in the sand, the clumps of coral and, moving rhythmically along, his own shadow.

As he swam Miago remembered the silver conch and how close he'd come to drowning. He wondered at the price one would fetch at market and the fame it would bring him. They'd say it was an omen and that he brought good luck – perhaps the fishermen would then fight to carry him in their canoes? He thought of the little dolphin. *Why were you alone? You should have been swimming in a family group.* He thrust himself higher and scanned the wave tops as he wondered in what part of the ocean it was swimming today.

Below him a shell lay in a patch of sunlight. He filled his lungs and dived but when he was closer, he saw it was empty. A crab claw and broken sea urchin spines lay beside it. He studied the reef and part of it moved, then darkened. Nodules formed that matched the surrounding coral. You're lucky the canoe has gone, he thought, or I'd get my harpoon Mr Octopus. He was turning for the surface when, from the corner of his eye, he saw a long shadow drift across the octopus's lair. He looked again but the shadow was gone.

Miago went with the current. Below him a spotted stingray flapped its wings and settled beneath a cloud of sand. He was tracking a school of fusiliers when, again, something moved at the very edge of his vision field. At first Miago thought he'd imagined it. Perhaps a cloud was playing tricks with the light but as he peered into the place where the yellows and blues merged with indigo, he saw it again.

Miago slowed his beating limbs. If it was what he feared, he didn't want to send out signals. He checked the surface but saw nothing. He raised his body higher and searched again.

A dark triangle sliced the wave tops. Miago saw the disturbance caused by the sweep of the tail and when he measured the distance between the fin and the tail, he gasped. Because it was bigger than any shark he'd ever seen.

Why was it so close to the reef? Was it hunting for dead animals washed down from the forest? Had it come this way because it was bored with patrolling the waters off Offal Rock?

What Miago did know was that they called it the Striped Death and that some tribes worshipped it as a god but to him

it was no god. It was a merciless killer that took fish and birds, turtles and men.

Miago lost it in the glare of the sun. He studied the sand, searching for its shadow, checking every angle. Finally he guessed the shark had moved back to the deeps, so he relaxed a little. One final look and he pushed it from his mind.

The seabed was rich with shells and his sack was filling. He wondered how he could dive deeper and stay submerged for longer. Maybe he could hollow out a bamboo and use it to breathe through?

Then Miago saw the shadow again but it was closer. He cursed himself for not being more careful. The shark may have moved away but his splashing had summoned it once more.

Miago inhaled sharply when he saw the length of the gently flexing shape. It was side-on, circling him. A pulse of fear swept through him that heightened his senses and sickened his stomach. As part of him froze, another part wanted to drop his bag and stick and swim for it but he knew that panicking was the worst thing he could do.

Miago's world closed around him. There was no reef or village, no ceremony or girl. The current had carried him too far from the canoe and this final drama would be played out in a prison cell that shrank with each circle of the shark. As time slowed, he asked himself: *why me? Why now?*

The waves danced over the shark's broad head, splitting the black eye that watched him into a dozen fragments. The distortion took in the gills and confused the banding down the muscular side. Miago couldn't see the underslung mouth or the rows of jagged teeth but they were there in the nightmare of his imagination. He saw the way the shape was banking as the circles tightened and its speed rose. Certain now that he would die, he prayed it would be over quickly.

Another feeling began to emerge. It was anger, anger that this was happening to him when his life was unresolved. A voice told him to fight back. He would die but he would die fighting. Perhaps he could gouge out an eye or reach into its gills and rip something out?

Desperately Miago tried to remember what he knew about these sharks. There was one it had taken four men to kill, drag ashore and butcher. Its huge head, the muscled body, the gasps when the undigested baboon had flopped onto the sand. But this one was bigger. He found himself thinking of the Maker and the fighting fisherman. Hadn't the Maker said something about not meeting strength with strength?

The shark was closer. As if in a dream, Miago remembered a story his grandfather had told him years before. It involved a ritual, an ordeal faced by the young men of a distant island. Those who passed the test became warriors because it demonstrated timing and bravery.

Miago raised the claw-stick. Could he fend the beast off? It was circling faster now and the stick was unwieldy. He aimed at the shark's flank, hoping a sharp thrust would frighten it away. To his dismay, the blow glanced off the monster's back.

As the great expanse slipped past he saw the slats it breathed through and the bulge of water pushed by its head. He moaned as he pictured himself held at the waist, crushed and broken, like a rat shaken by a dog. He dropped the sack and claw-stick and reached for the knife.

Twisting, Miago saw the spray thrown by the shark's sickle tail and the dark of its back lighten as it rolled. His world became the cavernous mouth and serrated teeth. Miago saw its eye slip behind a protective layer of skin. In that second, as the jaws targeted him, Miago knew it was blind.

He flung himself sideways and, with both hands locked on the knife, thrust down on the passing belly. The tough hide didn't yield and for seconds he balanced on the tip of the blade. Panicking, he locked his arms and pushed harder. He was lifted clear of the water. Then it went in.

Miago was blinded by an explosion of bubbles. The knife buried itself knuckle-deep and he ground it deeper until his fingers were mixed with the slippery warmth of the shark's insides. He gripped the handle with all his strength as the shark's momentum dragged it along the blade. There was a grotesque ripping sound as it sliced the soft organs inside. A spray of dark blood and green bile spattered his face. When the knife lodged in the spine, Miago threw himself sideways to avoid the frantic sweeps of the tail.

A dark stain spread from the pumping gills. The shark floated belly up and Miago looked into the black eye. Then the monster began to twitch and convulse, as if its muscles were trying to expel the knife. As he watched, its jaws began a hideous snapping that took in water, air and its own blood. It thrashed and rolled, the water its tail threw was now pink and, as Miago drifted with it, the reef stilled to watch.

Miago felt no triumph because he knew the blood would bring more sharks and that the canoe was too far away. So he trod water gently, praying he'd be ignored by the other predators that in his imagination, now circled him.

The reef stirred. Where the bloody cloud sank to the coral, the colourful fish – the angels and parrots, the butterflies and tangs – moved from cover to sift it for crumbs. Miago saw a hovering barracuda that stalked them. In a blink it was gone, a snapper vanishing in a flash of silver. A school of jacks, bold

and hungry, patrolled the stained water as the shark ground on its imaginary meal.

Miago's mind was locked in the rawness of nature. He'd become an observer, an outsider trapped in a drama he longed to escape. He'd defeated a great beast, a creature sent by evil spirits to devour him. Though somehow he'd triumphed ... he felt no joy in victory. Because whoever had sent the shark would now be angry.

The lapping waves had carried the news down current to a pod of reef sharks. They ghosted in, their speed and numbers building. A streak of grey and the pack leader drove its head into the bleeding wound. There was grinding and crunching as the water boiled and foamed. Rolling, the reef shark broke free and the ragged cube it held vanished in a gulping swallow. Streaming a bloody trail, it dived as its companions attacked.

Treading water, Miago avoided the spreading bloodstain. The dead shark twitched as its attackers tore at its belly then ripped out its heart. Miago was held by its black eye that was unchanged in death. He never saw the canoe that drew alongside or heard the shouts of its occupants. He didn't feel them lift him aboard or taste the water they gave him. There was laughter and shouts of delight. They gasped at his bravery, they clapped him on the back and they sang. But Miago was only aware of his shivering and, as he stared into nothing, the vomiting started.

Miago watched as they lashed the carcass to the outrigger. He saw one man beat off the reef sharks with a paddle, another who stabbed at them with a harpoon. He still felt sick and cared little that they were heading home. They needed his help when they pulled the beast ashore but he didn't notice its weight or feel the rough-textured skin. A crowd gathered and the fishermen measured the carcass; they argued and checked their findings. An old man was summoned because he'd seen many sharks but never one like this. Miago heard someone suggest it had been sent by the Goddess of Fire and Thunder as a test; another claimed it had been attracted from the deeps by the recent eclipse.

In silence Miago watched as the shark's jaws were hacked out and placed on a fire ant mound. Its spine was removed and trimmed of flesh. The fins were sliced off and left to dry in the sun. Cubes of meat were removed and the entrails were saved for the fish traps; the skin was ripped off for sandpaper. In time Miago saw how little was left for the crabs and birds, or for the monitor lizards that emerged with flickering tongues from the forest.

Miago was carried shoulder-high by the excited crowd. He was jostled and tugged, and a woman whispered something about meeting her daughter. But he didn't want this. He wanted only to escape, to be alone, but now the crowd was praising him in song that became a chant: "Carve Miago's name on the Sun Stone!" Miago recognized a Thinker who stopped to record the event in writing; he saw a group of Believers withdraw to pray.

The throng had a life of its own and suddenly it moved on without him. As the voices faded, Miago found himself alone in the Ceremonial Square. He breathed deeply to rid his body of tension. He told himself to be grateful he'd survived but when he looked around, his problems flooded back.

Three black flagpoles rose before him. He saw where the vines had crept from the forest and a mudslide that had demolished a section of wall where a dog was sniffing for food. He knew that soon they would hack away the vines and sweep the square before woven mats were laid on the stone seating. The timbered arch would be repainted in black and flower petals would be scattered by singing women. Miago imagined the Men of Knowledge climbing the dais to address the expectant crowd.

His gaze fell on a great totem that shone in lacquered ebony. Four sacred trees had been spliced together, and he knew how only hand-picked artisans had been permitted to work the shells and stones into the dark timber. Way up high, giant clams formed glaring eyes beneath a trio of carved vultures. The totem was adorned with skulls, and the hair that sprouted from them glistened with the resin that coated it. From the gaping mouth Miago watched the fabric tongue that flapped like a dolphin's tail on the evening breeze.

Miago's stare settled on the cages that hung from the totem's arms, and on the bones within. He thought of the family that had escaped, of the Trackers who dragged them back in chains ...

he heard again the cries for mercy and the clank of iron as the bolts were rammed home. A wave of nausea washed through him when he remembered the stench of rotting flesh and the vultures as they thrust their heads into the bloated corpses. The sickness was replaced by fury at the Men of Knowledge who had decreed the villagers file past the cages that dripped maggots under a baking sun. He looked at the banked-up skulls that encircled the totem's base and his hatred shifted. "Filthy Moroks," he whispered. He moved closer, lifting a child's skull that fitted snugly in his hand. It made him think of Cufu and he threw it against the totem. A sob escaped. "The lives of these Moroks count for nothing compared with your life, my brother!"

A noise made him turn and he saw that the dog was now digging. While he watched it, his mind slipped back in time. He filled the square with children and surrounded them with their families. The picture came easily because it had burned its way into his memory and on it settled a black cloud of apprehension. Miago relived the fear, the murmured expectation and misery. He saw again the pressing throng and the scared, staring faces. He imagined the line of cloaked and hooded figures that faced the crowd. He let last year's speeches return because he preferred to delay the next image: the handles of the marking irons that poked from the glowing brazier.

Miago tried to think of something positive about this year's ceremony. Maybe they would announce a new holiday or reduce the penance. If nothing else, it was a fine spectacle: there were the ceremonial clothes of the villagers, the fluttering flags and the brightness of the soldiers' armour. But then he recalled two guards restraining a sobbing, struggling girl. Miago winced as he remembered the Man of Knowledge lowering the glowing brand. He heard again the girl's pitiful screams.

Miago was running but the dog was faster. It came past him in a blur of tan, a possum locked in its jaws. He was still running when the dog dropped the twitching meal in front of its puppy.

Miago finally slowed in the lengthening shadows on the beach. He studied a great slab of rock where someone had scratched the shark's silhouette and he asked himself if anything

had really changed. Maybe he should claim that Banakaloo-Piki had spoken to him in a dream and told him he must kill it to release the village from bondage. But he knew this was dangerous because the Men of Knowledge would ask her their own questions.

The voice that interrupted his thoughts had a softness that caught him off guard. "Miago, I'm not sure what to say ..."

Miago expected T'lu-i to say how big the shark was, how brave he had been, how it was incredible that he'd killed it with only a knife but her words meant more to him.

"Miago, are you ... all right?"

He wasn't prepared. Something swelled in his throat. He wanted to speak but he was shaking now and only a squeak escaped. Embarrassed and angry, Miago turned away.

T'lu-i moved closer and put an arm around him. After a few steps she rested her head on his shoulder. His world became the softness of her hair and the scent of flowers. She whispered, "Come on. Let's get you home."

They walked in silence until Miago's pace slowed.

"What's wrong?" T'lu-i asked.

"Let's go the other way."

She hesitated. "You know we aren't allowed near the palace at night."

"But it'll be all right." Miago listened for noises. "No one's around."

They skirted a line of sandstone blocks and a pile of rubble to arrive at the palace wall. Behind it rose the tower.

"It's so elegant." Miago said.

"The only one still standing ..." T'lu-i murmured.

Serpent-like, a strangling vine encircled its cracked stonework.

"I think its days are numbered," Miago whispered.

A black and pitted boulder rested on a section of crushed

wall. The moonlight lit a courtyard beyond.

"Can you believe the Goddess's strength?" asked T'lu-i as she ran her fingers over the boulder.

"Or her anger?" Miago added.

She looked around. "We must leave, Miago."

But he didn't move. "I've always wanted to go in there," he said suddenly.

T'lu-i pulled his arm. "You know it's forbidden!"

"I'm going to climb that tower."

She gasped as he jogged past the boulder and scrambled over some rubble. T'lu-i hesitated. "I must be mad," she giggled nervously as she ran after him.

They crept into the courtyard. Miago stopped, his back pressed to the wall. T'lu-i leaned against him and he took her arm. She shivered. "It's cold in here."

Miago studied the interlocking blocks that formed the tower. He ran a finger along a joint. "Such craftsmanship – you couldn't fit a knife blade between these blocks."

She nodded. "No one builds like that now."

"That's true." He stepped forward.

"Miago, we can't climb it. It's not safe!"

"Come on. It'll be fine." The door groaned on rusty hinges. He pulled T'lu-i through the gap as she dragged in a lungful of air. "Don't hold your breath," he whispered.

"I always forget to breathe when I'm terrified!"

Miago felt a tightening of his chest but he knew she was depending on him. He tried to sound confident. "There's nothing to worry about."

They waited, allowing their eyes to adjust to the darkness.

"Did you see those hinges?" Miago asked. "They were shaped like dolphins."

"I love dolphins," T'lu-i whispered. "It's so … musty in here."

Ahead rose the steps of a spiral staircase. Miago liked the way T'lu-i stayed close to him. He studied the wall. "There were carvings here but they've been smashed by someone. It must have been so beautiful."

"Why would anyone do that?" T'lu-i asked with a shiver.

"Protect me, Miago!"

It was a chance to prove himself to her and for a moment his fear was gone.

As they climbed, the stairwell was lit by shafts of moonlight that penetrated the viewing ports. Miago slowed to check for spiders and bats. "There are five small steps then a big one. Then it's repeated. Why?"

"I was wondering that," said T'lu-i.

When they emerged at the top, he put his arm around her.

"What a view!" T'lu-i gasped, forgetting to whisper. "There's Banana Beach. Turtle Bay is behind that headland."

"Even at night Offal Rock is hidden by cloud," Miago said.

"That's strange – look at the water around it."

"I can see," he said.

"It's glinting."

"Is it the waves breaking on the reef?"

"I don't know. Or the moonlight playing on the coral?"

T'lu-i pointed. "My house is over there. There's yours."

Something else had caught Miago's attention. "Look what we're standing on. There's a pattern carved on the floor."

T'lu-i stared until she could make out the shape. "It's the layout of the old palace. Look!"

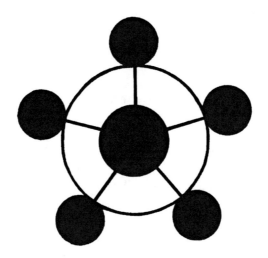

Together they followed the outline of the broken walls. T'lu-i pointed. "There were five outer towers – we're standing on one – and a bigger central tower. You can still make out the shapes."

"Yes, you're right. But why design a palace like that? Could it mean something?"

T'lu-i screwed up her face in concentration. "It's like the steps. Five small ones, then a big one."

"Was five an important number for our ancestors?" Miago asked.

When she didn't answer, he allowed his imagination to take over. "It must have been amazing. A palace of magnificent towers, a temple of pink marble ..."

"They say people visited the Palace of Peace from all corners of the world," T'lu-i sighed. "They came seeking guidance, they left contented."

Miago sighed. "So what did our ancestors do that was so wrong? Why did the Great Goddess destroy them?"

They stared in silence, absorbing every detail. The walls were topped with diamond-shaped crenellations, the inner courtyard was paved in stone. In one corner a candle flickered on a wooden table.

Miago pointed. "What are those things leaning against the wall?"

T'lu-i peered into the darkness. "I can't really see. Weapons?"

Miago squinted. "There are some spears by that ..." He shuddered.

"Is that what I think it is?" she asked.

He spoke slowly, his voice deep and cold. "Yes. It's the brazier."

"There are three handles coming out of it. Those must be the markers."

"I think branding irons describes them better," Miago hissed.

They jumped back when a door suddenly opened. A cloaked figure stepped into the courtyard. He was carrying something. He dropped it on the table where it landed with a thump.

"What's that?" T'lu-i whispered.

"Shhh. Keep still." Miago gasped, "His hood's down." Miago remembered the warning: you will go mad if you see the face of a Man of Knowledge. "Whatever you do, don't look at him!"

"I, I already have but it's so dark ..."

Miago also dared to look and a shiver ran through him. His voice quivered. "I can't really see him from here."

"I think that *him* could be a *her*!" T'lu-i whispered.

Miago stared. "Why do you say that?"

She nudged him. "Her hair's as long as mine!"

Miago concentrated. "It is? It looks ... short to me."

Miago knew how quietly they'd spoken, but now the cloaked figure was looking around. The Man of Knowledge lifted his head and they heard sniffing.

Miago whispered. "Can he *smell* us?"

Slowly the head turned left, then right. It stopped, facing the tower. Miago held his breath. Their quickening heartbeats merged as the figure seemed to stare straight at them. A trickle of sweat worked down Miago's back. Slowly the Man of Knowledge walked around the table and approached the tower.

Miago's squeezed T'lu-i hand and he felt its cold wetness. He screamed at himself: *you fool, you stupid fool … if only we'd gone home!*

The cloaked figure now stood at the base of the tower where he paused to sniff again. He stepped towards the door.

T'lu-i moaned in terror. "He knows we're here!"

They backed against the parapet.

Moments later came the scrape of leather on stone and rasping breaths as the Man of Knowledge worked his way, step by step, up the tower.

They stood transfixed, dreading the emergence of the cloaked figure. It took all Miago's strength to force the words out. "Whatever you do, don't look at his face! Let me take the blame!"

T'lu-i sobbed. "No, we're in this together."

They jumped as a harsh voice split the night air. "Where are you? What are you doing? We must hurry before the fools find out." Miago stared across the courtyard where a second Man of Knowledge now stood.

The footsteps stopped. When they started again, they were descending. The Man of Knowledge emerged at the base of the tower. He glanced up again before walking back to join his companion. He picked up what he had dropped earlier.

T'lu-i whispered frantically, "What *is* that, Miago?"

"I can't see," he replied, craning his neck.

The Man of Knowledge began to wrap the object in a long strip of dark cloth. He moved the candle closer to check his work and then he blew it out. Throwing the package over his shoulder, he moved off with his companion. Miago and T'lu-i watched them duck under a low door and through a gap in the wall.

T'lu-i frowned. "That's not the way back to the village. He must have made a mistake. That path leads to the volcano."

Miago waited until they were out of sight. He spoke coldly, "The Men of Knowledge don't make mistakes."

TERMITE AND BLOWFISH

The dawn silence was broken by the stamping of feet, the clatter of armour and by shouting. The soldiers had come for him.

Miago lay trembling in bed. "Now what trouble have you got yourself into?" Thunder Fly bellowed as he burst into Miago's room.

Miago could hear his mother pleading with the soldiers. "He's a good boy. I'm sure he has done nothing wrong."

Miago jumped out of bed and threw his tunic over his shoulders. He smiled at his mother before facing the soldiers. One was short, with darting eyes that were set in a pinched, angular face. His skin had a strange coppery hue and, where his hair escaped from beneath the helmet, Miago saw hints of orange. The soldier's uniform was too big so that his body seemed to move independently of it. The other was a whale of a man, with kinder eyes and a crushed nose that forced him to breathe through his mouth, his cheeks filling and emptying like bellows. His chest rose and fell too, imprisoned in a uniform that looked several sizes too small.

"Hello, Termite and Blowfish," Miago said, hoping to sound unconcerned.

Termite glared at him. "You're coming with us, boy."

"Don't worry," Miago whispered to his mother. "I'll be fine." He squeezed her hand.

"Spare me the long goodbyes," Termite mocked.

"He is so young to be summoned before the Supreme Council," his mother sobbed. "Perhaps one of his parents could accompany him."

"Impossible," shouted Termite. He shoved Miago. "Move!"

Blowfish shrugged. His tone was more sympathetic. "I don't think they execute children."

"There's always a first time," Termite hissed.

As they marched, Miago noticed the black cockatoo feathers that sprouted from their bronze helmets. Short chopping swords swung at their waists and from their arms hung black shields rimmed with bronze. Their glistening spear tips warned of stonefish venom.

Miago tried to push his fears away. Just my luck, he thought – escorted by two of our finest guards. He wondered why no one had suggested they swap uniforms. He laughed to himself; no wonder they were Workers! But his humour evaporated when he remembered where they were taking him.

They marched at speed in the dawn light, passing the broken houses, the tumbled walls. The street was empty but for the sleeping dogs. Overhead a fruit bat flapped silently home to roost. Turning a corner they met a gang of men, tethered by their chained ankles. Miago saw the rocks they passed between them. A guard shouted, "When you scum have filled that crack in the road, we'll find you another! Then another!"

Termite turned to Miago. "If you're lucky they'll put you to work. If *I'm* lucky, I'll get to guard you!"

They were closing on a long building. In the half light the carved columns gave it a presence that was lost when Miago saw the angle of the roof, the collapsed doorway and the fractured stonework. *My god we're nearly there. Think you fool!* He searched for an explanation and remembered the shark. Perhaps the Supreme Council wanted to reward him? But reality soon returned: *you've been summoned because you were seen last night.*

"So, boy," Termite said with relish. "You must be in serious trouble for them to send us. I heard their meeting started at sunset."

"I'm glad it's not me they've summoned," Blowfish added.

Termite's eyes narrowed. "Tell us what you've done. If you confess, they might be lenient." After a pause he added, "And torturing children can be so … noisy!"

Miago wondered who had seen them climb the tower. He tried to sound convincing. "I don't know why they've summoned me. I really don't!"

A shrill laugh escaped from Termite. "The young fool can't

say we didn't try to help."

"Don't even think of lying because they can tell," Blowfish advised. "If I was you, I'd admit everything from the start."

Their pace quickened as they neared the Great Chamber. Termite pushed Miago inside and marched him to a ring of candles. Blowfish bellowed "Halt!" then the soldiers bowed before shuffling back, their spears levelled to block Miago's escape.

It was early and with little natural light filling the chamber, Miago's eyes adjusted slowly. The first things he saw were the sun ports that were blocked with vegetation and hardened lava. Beyond, more candles flickered on mounds of broken masonry. There were cracked columns with faded paintwork and stone carvings were scattered across the floor. Miago saw chipped marble and dark patches where the forest mud had oozed in.

The walls were decorated with mosaics depicting ocean and jungle scenes but they were cracked and stained. Before him stood an armless statue; another, of a mother and child lay locked in combat with a tree root. At the end of the chamber the half-light revealed a number of shapes: men seated, stock-still, around a table. Their faces were lost beneath their hoods. When he realized they all faced him, Miago trembled.

He wanted something to lean on. As his legs weakened, he wished he could sit down. Cold beads of sweat formed on his forehead and his hands felt clammy but something told him not to wipe them on his tunic. He mouthed his mantra, "Show no weakness."

When the voice came, he jumped but the tone sounded kind enough. "So, young man, they tell me you're the one who killed the shark. I saw its jaws. A remarkable achievement! And all you had was …" the man picked something up, and Miago saw how the blade glinted dimly in the half-light, "… this knife. Not very big, is it?"

Miago relaxed a little. "But it's strong and sharp, sir."

"It must be. Where did it come from?"

"I was given it."

"By whom?"

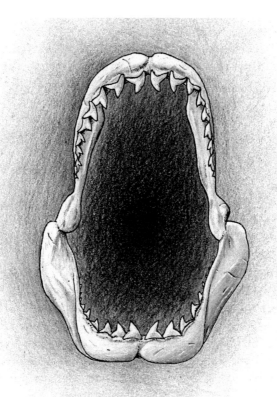

"Monkey Blood, sir."

"Ah, the one with the … unsatisfactory marking." The Man of Knowledge studied the knife. "These crosses on the handle.

Are they your work?"

"No, sir."

"Do you know who made them?"

Miago shook his head. There was whispering from the table. "Why would anyone do that to a good knife?" the Man of Knowledge asked.

"Perhaps they are kill marks?" Miago suggested. "May I have it back, sir?"

"Hold your tongue, boy!" A sweep of the arm, and the knife was embedded in the table. When the words came again, they came slowly. "Perhaps you could explain why you were swimming near Offal Rock."

Miago tensed. "Offal Rock? I never went near it, sir. I swear!"

"Are you quite sure, boy?"

Miago couldn't control the fear in his voice as his words hung in the silence. "Yes sir."

"While swimming, perhaps you looked up at it? Tell us what you saw."

Miago knew he had to be very careful. "I was nowhere near it," he repeated. "The shark swam up current of me."

"I did not ask you about the shark. I asked you what you saw."

Miago answered quickly. "I saw nothing, sir. Only mist and cloud. Then I looked away."

A deeper voice joined in. "And if the mist and cloud had parted, what would you have seen?"

"They say it's a small island of jagged rocks," said Miago without hesitation. "No plants or trees, just huge beetles that hunt for dead things left by the tide and, and great spiders that spin webs in the shallows for any man the sharks miss." He shivered. "The island's cursed. It attracts only death."

"What about the reef there? You must know the stories?"

Miago spoke carefully. "People say it can shine brightly."

"And have you seen it shining, boy?"

Miago remembered how, when he was standing on the tower with T'lu-i, the reef had glinted in the moonlight. He also remembered Blowfish's warning that the Men of Knowledge could tell if you were lying.

"Answer me boy!"

"No, sir."

Miago stood in silence. *Do they believe me? Why won't they say something?*

Finally the Man of Knowledge spoke. "Why boy, would a reef shine?"

"It must be a trap. To lure sailors onto it."

"Good." It was the first voice again. "I'm glad you understand never to trespass there and that it's dangerous even to look. Because we would find out. You know that, don't you?"

"Yes, sir," Miago whispered.

After a pause, "Perhaps you could explain how a boy of your age could kill so large a shark?"

Miago collected his thoughts. "I remembered a story my grandfather told me, sir."

"What story?"

"He heard it from a stranger long ago. It was about a ritual on a distant island and how to kill those sharks."

"Did your grandfather describe this stranger?"

That's a strange question. "No sir."

Slowly another figure rose. The cloaked arm pointed at Miago. "Who is the stranger you have been seen with?"

Miago swallowed "He's called ... the Maker, sir."

"The Maker? And why is he called that?"

"Because he makes things." Miago realized he might have sounded insolent. "I mean, he collects things. I've given him cowries for a belt, he took a broken triton away. I've seen him with macaw feathers ..."

"So he collects shells and feathers?" There was more whispering. "What did you talk to him about?"

Miago hoped they couldn't see his face too clearly. "Very little, sir. I know I'm not allowed to ask outsiders questions. He only wanted some shells." Miago's voice tailed off. He inhaled deeply, searching for courage. *How many more questions do they have?*

There was a pause before a new voice joined in, one that rasped and wheezed, and Miago had to concentrate to understand the words. "Boy, you look familiar. Are you the one who used to have visions?"

Miago spoke carefully. "Yes sir but they stopped when I lost my brother."

"You remember my advice?"

"To tense my muscles and shout!"

"Good. You see, we always know what's best."

"I know that, sir."

The Man of Knowledge spoke again but this time so slowly that Miago knew to be on guard. "What I want to know is this: the one you call the Maker ... and the stranger who spoke to your grandfather ... do you suppose they are one and the same?"

Miago was confused. "I don't think so. The Maker isn't old enough."

"But you just said your grandfather didn't describe him. Now you seem to know his age."

"I'm sorry sir, I meant ..." Miago's answer died on his lips as he searched for something to say. "Forgive me, I'm confused."

"I will make this question as simple as I can: how old is the Maker?"

"I don't know. He has a grey beard but his eyes are young."

"And, boy, what else do you know about him?"

"Nothing, sir."

"Not even where he comes from?"

Miago flinched. How could the Man of Knowledge know that he had asked the Maker that very question? *Think, Miago!* Maybe asking where an outsider comes from is the most natural question in the world.

Miago started slowly. "I did ask him but his answer made

no sense."

"Which was?"

"He said something about coming from somewhere close that's very far away."

"What do you think he meant by that?"

Miago played the words back slowly but he couldn't understand them. "Somewhere can't be close and far away at the same time. So I think he likes to play games with words."

There was silence. A Man of Knowledge who had not spoken now approached Miago. The hood served its purpose well. All Miago could see beneath it was shadow. He found himself moving back until he felt the heat of a candle on his calf.

This voice was deliberate and slow. It sounded as if the man's throat was full of phlegm because he gurgled as he spoke. "I would be ... disappointed if reports reached us that you had been seen with the Maker again."

"I, I understand, sir."

"And that other man, Monkey Blood. He sets a bad example. Avoid him too."

"Yes sir."

There was silence so Miago decided to chance his luck. "May I ask, sir, what the Maker has done?"

The shapes at the table huddled closer together. There was more whispering. Then the rasping voice spoke. "We have received news that an advance party of Moroks have set up camp on the plain beyond the forest. He is obviously one of their spies."

Miago imagined the Morok camp. He saw the black skins that covered their tents and giant, unruly horses. Dogs howled; the air was thick with flies as tangle-haired women beat their whimpering children. There were dark, shadowy figures that spoke in whispers, and caged prisoners. His imagination added fighting and drunkenness to the stench of rotting food and excrement.

A Man of Knowledge lifted something from under the table. "I believe this belonged to your brother." He motioned to Blowfish. "Give it to the boy."

Blowfish walked to the table. He bowed, and turned back

to Miago, throwing the object at him. Miago caught it. It had worn patches and a torn ear. A clump of straw protruded from a hole in its head. He couldn't believe his eyes. "Cufu's stuffed possum!" Without thinking, Miago lifted it to his nose. It even smelt the same.

"The soldier who found it said its name was Bok Bok. Is that correct?"

"Yes, sir," Miago whispered. "Where did he find him?"

"Near the Morok camp. By killing the shark you have earned the right to have it back and finally – "

They were interrupted by a commotion outside. Miago could hear shouting and a woman's hysterical sobbing. A soldier burst in and bowed before running to the table.

"You dare interrupt us?"

The soldier leaned forward and whispered something.

"I see. How unfortunate." The Man of Knowledge dismissed the soldier and turned back to Miago. "I have just learned that the Moroks came last night. They took another child. This will not go unpunished. We shall set fresh traps and send out a patrol in two days. You will be on that patrol. If you are lucky, you will kill a Morok. That way you can prove yourself to us. It will help you make your Life Choice, avenge your brother and bring honour to your family."

Miago raised his head. "Thank you, sir," he said fiercely. "Thank you!"

"Now go."

He ran home and burst into the house. His mother hugged him, and his sister bombarded him with questions as his father glared at them in silence.

They asked why the Supreme Council had summoned him, what had been said. He had prepared his answer but first he showed them Bok Bok. He spoke carefully. "The Men of Knowledge talked about the Moroks. They're sending me on a patrol to check the traps." His voice changed pitch. "If the soldiers catch one, I shall have the honour of killing him."

Miago sat on the end of the bed. He placed Bok Bok gently beside him. His thoughts slipped back in time.

It was low tide as he stepped onto the mud. He squatted to study the jungle of mangrove roots. "Come on, Cufu," he called. "Bring the box and watch out for snakes."

Cufu hesitated. "Mud too smelly. Smell like … and Bok Bok no like. Me put him in tree."

"Come on, it's fine," Miago said. "It washes off, I promise."

But Cufu was preoccupied. "Bok Bok got hole in tail. Miago fix?"

"Yes, I'll fix him again," Miago laughed. "You sure it's only one hole this time?"

Cufu pointed. "Crab!" he said hopefully. "Catch him quick!"

"That's a hermit crab. We don't want those." Moments later, "Here's something. Bring the box, Cufu! I've found one."

Cufu pouted. "Me no like mud! Why crabs live in mud?"

Miago laughed. "That's why they're called mud crabs! Bring the box if you want to eat tonight."

"But crabs taste of mud," Cufu glowered.

"No. They taste good," Miago said. "If you help me, tomorrow I'll show you my secret place in the forest. We can play armies."

Cufu stepped forward and wailed as he sank in the mud. "Stuck!" he cried. "Help! Cufu stuck!"

"Hold the stick, that's it." Miago pulled Cufu out. "You see the hole by that mangrove?"

Cufu nodded suspiciously.

"Our crab's in there," Miago explained. "When he comes out, hold him round the back like I showed you."

Cufu didn't move as the mud crab, claws raised, edged from the hole. It scurried sideways.

"Quick, Cufu. You can do it!"

Cufu hid behind Miago. "Crab too big! Claws too big! Crab angry!" he said, his voice muffled in Miago's tunic. "Me scared."

"Go on, try. I'll protect you."

The scream made Miago jump.

"Him got me, crab bite Cufu!"

Miago moved quickly to prise the claw off his brother's finger. He checked it carefully. "It's not bleeding," he whispered to the sobbing child.

"You saved Cufu. Crab try kill me! He want eat me!"

"I shouldn't have let him nip you. I'm sorry."

Cufu's eyes were wide and the tears still flowed. His tone surprised Miago, "You save Cufu. One day Cufu save Miago."

Miago laughed. "That's what brothers are for."

Miago gently took Cufu's hand and together they placed the crab in the box. "Cufu, you're so brave!" He smiled as the small boy closed the lid, lifting the box proudly to his chest. "I couldn't have done that myself, Cufu. He's a very big one!"

"You tell Mama I caught him," said Cufu with contentment, trotting beside his brother. "I brave boy. I tell Bok Bok!"

Miago squeezed his shoulder and pointed. "I think there's another one over there. See the hole?"

"I get this one too!" Cufu said, grabbing Miago's stick. "Stand back. Cufu best crab catcher in world!"

They walked back laughing. When they reached home, Cufu stopped and tugged Miago's arm. Miago had never seen such concentration in his brother's face. "Cufu?"

"Cufu never forget promise to help Miago."

Miago repeated Cufu's words as he looked around his empty room. A terrible loneliness engulfed him as he wiped his eyes and walked to the window, staring out at nothing. He stayed there all morning.

THEY CAN'T LIVE FOREVER

In a few hours Miago would be going on patrol. He needed to be alone so he walked to the spot where they had butchered the shark. There was no stain on the sand now because the gulls and monitor lizards had picked the site clean. The wind and tides had done their work too, so much so that Miago began to wonder if he even had the right place.

Miago heard a noise and he turned, listening carefully. It sounded like something crashing through the vegetation, heading his way. A large animal? The noise grew louder and Miago knew it was too late to run so he jumped behind a tree. Suddenly a boy burst from the forest. He stopped and looked behind him.

Miago stepped from cover. "Why are you running, Damago?"

"Miago! Six Toes was chasing me!" he said, panting.

"Six Toes? He can't run very fast."

"He's quicker than you think but I lost him."

Why was he chasing you?"

"I don't know. What are you doing here, Miago?"

"I'm trying to work something out."

"Your Life Choice?"

Miago frowned. "No. I'm thinking about the night before the ceremony. I think I should cut an escape route in the jungle behind me. But if I do, how can I stop someone ... or some*thing* sneaking up it when I'm asleep?"

"Miago, if the gods want you to survive in the forest, you will. If they don't, then nothing you do will help."

"You would say that, Damago. What's that you're carrying?"

"Tarama root. It's just been decreed that this year we're allowed to rub it on the marks," he said, relief in his voice. "Banakaloo-Piki told a Man of Knowledge that it numbs the pain. Isn't that good news?"

"Did Six Toes see you digging it up?"

"Yes. Why?" Damago thought for a moment. He winked at Miago, "Oh, I think I understand ... he must use it in his fishing potion."

"We'd better not tell anyone. How do you prepare it?" asked Miago.

"You scrape off the bark and boil it until it's a thick paste. Let it cool and then rub it in."

"But can it ease the pain of making the wrong choice?"

"Oh, Miago! I'm looking forward to my adult life. It's the marking I'm scared of. I've never been good with pain. Ever since you tricked me with that animal you kept. What was its name?"

"Spiky." Miago laughed. "Have you still not forgiven me? That was years ago!"

Damago was inspecting his hand. "I learned you can stroke a porcupine from its head to its tail but you can't stroke it from its tail to its head. I still have the scars to prove it!"

Miago was silent.

"Miago?"

"You've just given me an idea. Yes, yes, I think I'll try it."

"What are you talking about?"

"Never mind."

"Miago, you think too much! Anyway, I like the idea of becoming a Believer. Who knows, one day I may even make Man of Knowledge!" He paused. "*Now* what's wrong?"

"When was the last time they created a new Man of Knowledge?"

"Not in my lifetime but they can't live forever."

Miago kept the thought to himself: *I'm not so sure.*

"I need to get back. See you at the ceremony," said Damago lightly. "And good luck cousin!"

Approaching the edge of the forest, Miago thought about how their lives would change before they talked again. He walked noisily through the fallen leaves to drive away any palm vipers. He pictured their coiled, camouflaged bodies and coffin-shaped heads. The bite that kills children and blackens men's legs. He picked up a stick and beat a path through the leaves.

He reached the fire ant mound. The shark jaw glowed white in the sun; not a speck of flesh remained. Miago lifted it and saw there were teeth missing. He shook it vigorously, dislodging a few ants as he spoke, "I love this place – people even steal my shark teeth." He dragged a stick across them. In seconds the wood was pulp.

The shark's spine stretched like a bleached bamboo across the mound. It too had been picked clean. Miago studied the knobbly vertebrae and noticed the gash left by the knife. He was reliving the battle with the shark when a voice interrupted his thoughts.

"I would like to make you an offer for some teeth and a few pieces of spine … and I need more shells."

The man wore a loose cotton garment decorated with simple motifs. A line of cowries was stitched to his belt; the leather pouch that hung from it was new. A hat made from coconut husk sat low on his head but the stick he leaned on was as familiar as his smile.

"I was hoping I'd see you again!" Miago said, delighted.

"Keep your voice down or we'll get in trouble. Do you like the belt?"

Miago felt a charge first of excitement, then of worry. "How did you know I'm not meant to talk to you?"

The Maker laughed. "Oh, I got in trouble last time I was here. Some things never change … hence the new clothes. This time I am a simple merchant who has crossed stormy oceans, swum crocodile-infested rivers and climbed belching volcanoes in search of … shark's teeth! But sadly I can still only pay you with words."

Miago's father had told him to keep the teeth as a souvenir and Market Man had offered to buy them. But Miago had a better idea. "They're yours. What will you use them for?"

"Boiled and mixed with crushed shell, the spine makes strong glue," the Maker said. "And I will slip a few pieces over this stick for decoration." He thought for a moment. "The teeth are good for jewellery. Perhaps I'll make something you can give T'lu-i."

Miago's voice softened. "It's good to see you again. I need someone to talk to."

The Maker smiled. "Well, not here. We must find somewhere we won't be seen."

"I know a place," said Miago.

As they hurried through the lower forest Miago turned to check that they weren't being followed. They passed the banana

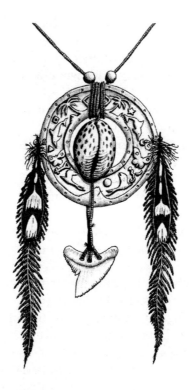

plantation and a field of tobacco plants, and stopped by a cinnamon tree. Miago peeled off a piece of bark. He rubbed it and held up his fingers. "This one's ready. I love the smell."

But the Maker stayed where he was. "I'm stuck," he said, a note of surprise in his voice.

"That's puncture vine," said Miago, hurrying over. "Don't struggle. You'll only make it worse."

The vine had wrapped around the Maker's sleeve, the razor thorns snaring the fabric. When he was free, the Maker studied his arm. "It cut me."

"You're lucky you weren't alone. I once found a deer caught in it. It had been struggling and was being smothered by it. I should have slit its throat and taken it back for food."

"What did you do?"

"I cut it free but it collapsed so I blew air into its lungs.

I washed its wounds and held it upright until its strength returned. Eventually, it made its way back into the forest."

"That was a good thing you did."

"It was so helpless and beautiful. Do you know what I'll never forget?"

"Tell me."

"Before it hopped away it turned and stared at me. I don't know whether it was trying to say thank you. But I'll never forget the look in its eyes."

They walked in silence. Finally the Maker spoke. "So what did they ask about me?"

"What your name was and how old you were. Where you came from." Miago felt a pang of guilt but with it excitement, the thrill of disobeying *them*.

"I bet they told you not to speak to the Maker again?"

"Yes?"

"Well, you must do as they command!"

"But –"

He chuckled. "So I will change my name and you won't be disobeying them."

Miago laughed and the Maker laughed too. "You know something, Miago, you should laugh more."

Miago wondered why his father couldn't be more like this man. He hadn't thought about it before but what the Maker said might be true; except that without Cufu in his life there had been little to laugh about. Ahead, a striped lizard crawled slowly along the path. Turning, it studied them through armoured eye sockets.

"It's changing colour," the Maker said. Sure enough, the lizard was losing its vivid stripes and the green was changing to brown until it blended with the soil.

"A chameleon," said Miago, glancing at the Maker. "You remind me of that lizard because you look so different. *That* can be your new name!"

The Maker seemed amused. "So now I'm the Chameleon, am I? I've been called worse. Where are you taking me anyway?"

"To a secret place," said Miago. "When I was younger, I used to play there with my brother."

"You have a brother?"

He ignored the question. "We won't be disturbed."

"What sort of games did you play?"

Miago shrugged.

"Sometimes it helps to talk."

Miago started slowly. "It was childish. We played soldiers. We built a dam and our armies fought over the water supply."

"Armies fighting over water doesn't sound childish to me."

They followed the rock face and arrived at a stream that gurgled through the forest. Miago pointed at a pile of rubble. "That was once a watchtower. They built them to warn of the approaching enemy."

The Chameleon sighed. "Or to welcome home friends?"

Miago looked at him. He was about to ask what he meant but he stopped himself. *He's only playing games again.*

They came to a small clearing that was bordered by a bamboo thicket. A purple dragonfly hovered overhead. The Chameleon sat with his back resting against a bamboo. "Something on your mind, Miago?"

He paused before answering. "I'm going on patrol tonight to kill a Morok."

"How does that make you feel?"

"Excited!"

The Maker studied him closely. "Is that what's troubling you?"

"Nothing's troubling me."

"Look me in the eye and say that."

But Miago looked down. "The Men of Knowledge say you're a spy," he said quietly.

"Oh. Is that all?"

He was facing the Chameleon again. Before he knew it, he'd spoken his thoughts. "They, they tell me I shouldn't trust you. But I do."

"Thank you," said the Chameleon. "Trust is important."

"But T'lu-i's father says never trust anyone and he's the richest man in the village," Miago countered.

"Is he the one who sells knives to the young men?"

Miago shook his head. "T'lu-i hates knives. He wouldn't sell them behind her back."

"Does he have a limp?"

"Yes. He trod on a palm viper."

"That's him."

"You mean …?" Miago had watched Market Man haggling with customers until he'd secured the best price. They said he always extracted impossibly good deals from suppliers and that he drove other traders out of business. His competitors complained that he knew what people wanted to buy before they did. But now any respect Miago had felt for him had evaporated. His voice fell. "But she trusts him completely."

Miago had seen how T'lu-i always got what she wanted from her father. Often she'd boasted that *she* was *his* boss. Now he knew differently. "You mean he lets her think she's in charge when in fact it's all a lie?"

The Chameleon sighed. "Nothing else matters when money is your master."

"But she trusts him."

The Chameleon was silent.

"Tell me about trust."

Miago saw the mischief that played across the Chameleon's face. "I use glue to fix things. Sometimes I mix kimo gum with ground bone, or shark spine with tree sap. It depends … but the first thing I need is glue."

Miago frowned. "Why are you talking about glue?"

"Glue is like trust. You can't mend things without glue; you can't fix relationships without trust. Without it, society falls apart."

"I never thought of it like that." Miago remembered his people. "They've taught me that to trust anyone other than our rulers is a sign of weakness."

The Chameleon shrugged.

"Is the teaching wrong?"

The Chameleon laughed. "There are *fish*, Miago, that know more about trust than your people."

"Fish? You're making fun of me."

When the Chameleon didn't speak, Miago asked, "So you aren't working for the Moroks?"

The Chameleon held his eyes. "I was with them before I came here."

Miago recoiled. "So you *are* a spy!"

"Talking to someone doesn't make you a spy," said the Chameleon. "You know what? Everything you say about them, they say about you."

"But we're …"

The Chameleon raised his hand. "I know what you're going to say: that you're god's chosen people but the Moroks believe the same thing."

Miago's voice rose. "They can't be that stupid! You were in great danger in the Morok camp. They could've killed you!"

"I'm in greater danger here."

Miago's voice cracked. "You're confusing me again!" He stood and walked a short distance. He stopped and thought. His life was a mass of questions and from nowhere this strange man had arrived. He was the only person Miago could talk to but why must he speak in riddles? A wave of desperation swept through Miago. He spun round. "Please, I beg you – help me make my Life Choice!"

The Chameleon's voice flooded with sympathy. "Perhaps you're looking in the wrong place for answers?"

In his desperation, Miago now grew angry. "What does *that* mean?"

"People use their eyes to look out on the world," said the Chameleon. "What if you tried looking inside yourself? Left alone, most people become thinkers or workers or believers anyway. So why brand them?"

Miago was searching for something to say when the Chameleon laid a warm hand on his arm. "That's why so few men will ever know *tocamu*."

"What's that?" he asked wearily.

"An ancient word."

"What does it mean?"

"To know *tocamu*, you must undertake a journey."

"Where?"

"Inside yourself."

Miago laughed nervously. "How can you do that?"

The Chameleon sat silently so Miago searched for something to say. "If you could, what would you find?"

"You would meet someone," he voice deepened, "or something … that most people spend a lifetime avoiding. Men give it many names: the Dark Force, the Night Spirit. But it hides inside us all. The problem is that most men go blindly through life doing its work and they become greedy, selfish, cruel … they are not born that way."

Finally Miago spoke. "You've found your *tocamu*, haven't you? What did it feel like?"

The Chameleon pointed. "Imagine the forces at work deep inside the volcano. Think of the pressure that built up before the molten rock began to rise. Imagine it rushing up and bursting from the volcano. When it happens to a man, it can happen that way."

The Chameleon pointed at the branches of a tree where a bird sat. Miago saw its black and white plumage and long, colourful bill. "A toucan. So?"

As they watched a single feather drifted down, curling this way and that to land nearby. The Chameleon walked over and picked up the feather. He slipped it in his pouch. "The change can also be as gentle as a feather that settles silently in the forest." He scratched a shape in the sand:

"A butterfly?" Miago asked.

"Yes. It's a sacred sign."

"What does it mean?"

"What do you think it means, Miago?"

Miago thought. "Well, a caterpillar changes into a butterfly."

"Go on."

"And a butterfly is beautiful."

"And?"

"Unlike a caterpillar ... it can fly. Is that it?"

"Yes. The butterfly represents both the beauty we are blessed with and the gift of flight that we receive when we take the trouble to change ourselves."

"But people can't fly."

Miago saw that the Chameleon's attention had wandered. He was watching a piece of wood carried by the stream. He leaned forward and guided it to the bank with his stick. Lifting it, he studied its shape and the grain of the timber. "Exactly what I've been looking for," he said with satisfaction. "Thank you stream and tree for bringing me this fine gift."

"What do you want it for?" Miago asked.

The Chameleon shook the water off it and balanced it on his head. "How do I look?"

"Like a man with a lump of wood on his head."

"Where's your imagination?" the Chameleon admonished him with a smile.

Miago tried again. "A wooden helmet? That won't protect you here."

The Chameleon tucked the piece of wood under his arm. "I will say this, Miago. You don't realize it but you're close to knowing the answer to your Life Choice."

Miago felt a surge of frustration. "How can you say that when I'm less sure than ever?"

The Chameleon picked up the shark's jaw. He looked at the teeth and drew in his breath. "A very big one! But I've seen bigger."

He held up the jaws and framed Miago's head in them. When he spoke, it was with an intensity that Miago found disconcerting. "Recent events, Miago."

"Is it about the shark?"

"Go on."

"How I killed it. It was bigger and stronger than me ..."

"Yes?"

Miago felt the Chameleon's excitement. "I, I didn't try and match its strength, I let it charge past me and then I killed it."

"So you ...?"

"I used my brains to defeat its strength. Is that it?"

"And so ...?"

"There's more? But I don't understand. Please tell me!"

"As I said when we met, I will teach you how to ask questions but I won't give you answers."

"But there's so little time," Miago pleaded.

But the Chameleon said no more.

THE ENEMY

"Watch out for the Moroks," his father instructed Miago, adjusting his son's belt. "Beware of their poisons, and remember what I said about tracking them."

Miago was impatient to go but his father wasn't finished. "They're filthy and diseased," he said. "Don't breathe their air or touch them if you can help it."

"How do you say 'Die, Morok' in their language?" Miago asked.

His father snorted. "I don't know. Their language is very basic though I've heard they have twenty words for cow!"

Miago's mother had stitched new leather into his sandals. "Mudskipper, promise me you'll be careful?" she begged, enveloping him in a hug.

"Of course I will," he whispered. "And if I see any honey berries …"

She smiled through her tears. "Don't worry about those. Just promise to come back safely."

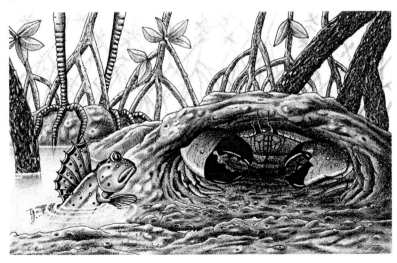

Miago jogged to the main square where a group of soldiers had assembled. They wore leather hunting armour, swords hung from their waists. Some carried spears, others bows. He knew that the full-face helmets had been designed for one enemy: Moroks. He smiled at a wiry looking soldier who was eyeing him with suspicion. "I wouldn't like to wear one of those helmets in this heat," Miago said.

"You'd rather have your eyes gouged out?"

Miago moved on, hoping to find a friendlier face. He saw how the men swaggered and boasted.

"I bet I'll get the first one, arrow at twenty paces, back of the head!" one shouted.

"You couldn't hit a house from there, Scar Neck!"

Another soldier was polishing his sword. "I've sharpened it as it's the start of the hunting season." He raised it admiringly. "Take a head off with one blow, this would."

One soldier was sitting with his back to Miago. His shoulders were huge and his flesh bulged through the gaps of his ill-fitting armour. "Scar Neck, have you dipped your arrows in poison?" the soldier asked. Miago recognized the gravelly voice. He walked forward.

"Hello, Blowfish."

The man turned. "Ah, my young friend," he said.

"Where's Termite?"

"Luckily he's off duty."

"You don't like him?"

"Does anyone?"

Miago caught another man's eye. The soldier grinned. "This is why I became a Worker. Hunting Moroks makes it all worthwhile!"

A tall, athletic officer motioned to Miago. "Are you the boy we must take with us?" he asked gruffly.

"Yes sir."

"My orders are that we must waste the first kill on you."

Miago hid a surge of excitement. "I know, sir."

"You'll do exactly as you're told. Keep in step, watch closely and don't get in the way. If you disobey or drop behind, you'll be abandoned in the forest. Understand?"

"Yes sir!"

"Form up, helmets on!" the officer bellowed.

They shuffled into two lines and, on command, set off at a fast pace. Miago struggled to match their stride pattern.

"Bring back ten skulls!" a woman shouted from a doorway.

"Avenge my daughter!" cried another.

They moved quickly through the lower forest. Where the path narrowed, the troop thinned to single file. They changed course when they reached the lower slopes of the volcano.

Miago turned to the soldier next to him. "I've never seen a Morok." His imagination took over. "Is it true they're huge and smell of rotting flesh? And they have strange eyes that –"

"No talking on patrol, boy!" the soldier snapped.

Miago flinched but the images kept coming and, with them, the excitement. *All my life I've heard about Moroks. I hope I finally see one because it will be a pleasure killing him ...*

They slowed as they entered a clearing. Miago stood back and watched the soldiers fan out. One of them, a small, wiry man, jogged forward and dropped onto all fours. He seemed to be studying a plant; he ran his fingers over its leaves and looked around slowly. Then he jumped up and advanced to a patch of thicker grass. He raised his spear and prodded the ground. Miago noticed how easily it pierced the soil.

"Well, Mongoose?" the officer asked.

"Trap's intact, sir."

"So's the gut, sir," said another soldier, studying the gap between two trees. "No one's been this way."

Miago felt a twinge of disappointment.

"Move out!" ordered the officer. "Pick up the pace; we have a lot of ground to cover."

Miago had never been this far into the forest. As they rounded a hillock and waded through shoulder-length sawgrass, he marvelled at the unfamiliar panorama that opened before him. He saw how the trees thinned to give way to knotted shrubs and barren patches of rock. The landscape slipped away in a series of undulations towards a distant plain. He tried to focus on the plain. Were people out there? Strange animals? But all he saw beneath a darkening sky was the deep green of the grassland and the brown meanders of a great river.

The officer pointed. "Somewhere on our grasslands, they skulk and they plot," he said, curling his lip. "Even now they could be watching us. Be on guard," he glanced at the setting sun, "because they are more active at night."

Did the Moroks hunt in packs like their dogs? Miago knew he was a strong swimmer but what use was that here? If the Moroks lived on the plains, they'd be good runners and how could he hope to outrun them? He imagined the dark shapes that blended with the rock and scrub. How effective would spears be against an invisible enemy? Would the soldiers' armour withstand a hail of poisoned darts? Would their helmets really protect them against a beast that leapt on their backs and drove sharpened talons into their eyes?

The next trap, a pit roofed with branches, leaves and topsoil, was well concealed. The grasses that covered it blended perfectly with their surroundings. "Trap's empty but ..." Mongoose knelt to inspect a stone. "Someone or something's been this way, sir."

"How can he tell?" Miago asked.

"Mongoose misses nothing," the soldier beside him said. Miago turned and was blasted by a cloud of rancid sweat. He backed away but the soldier and the smell followed him. "Mongoose could give a mouse a day's head start and still find him."

"But what's he looking for?"

"The sun dries things quickly. If you find a stone with its damp side facing up, it means it's been kicked over recently."

Miago heard Mongoose's excitement. "Gut's broken. A man's footprints, sir. Long toenails. Thin build, medium weight. Not a young man. Alone. Nervous. He was carrying something in his left hand. He may limp. " He pointed. "Went that way."

"How can he tell so much about him?"

The soldier shrugged. "Oh, he's good but he's no Tracker ..."

"What do you mean?" asked Miago.

"A Tracker could tell you the colour of the man's eyes.

Whether he was married, how many children he had. Even what he ate yesterday."

"Stop talking there," said the officer. "Weapons ready."

Miago whispered to the soldier beside him. "If you filled the trap with puncture vine …"

The man laughed coldly. "I like that idea!"

Miago was beginning to enjoy the atmosphere. He felt the tension building, the raw excitement of the hunt. He had done well so far and the soldiers seemed to accept him, so he moved on boldly searching for the next trap.

It was the unnatural angle of the sawgrass that caught his attention. "Over here!" he whispered.

"Good boy, you've found it!" The officer was at his shoulder. "And look! We've caught ourselves a filthy Morok!"

Miago imagined the muscular, crouching figure, eyes bulging, axe in hand waiting to spring up and attack. There would be a ghastly scream and bitter smell; the Morok would hack wildly until they cut him down. To his surprise, all he heard was whimpering.

A torch was thrust over the pit. At first it looked empty, but when Miago's eyes adjusted he made out the cowering shape in the corner. The Morok had wrapped his head in his hands and he was shaking. Miago saw the strange angle of a leg, the swollen knee.

"Well, well!" the officer drawled. "One Morok. Oh dear, he seems to have hurt his leg." He spun around. "Blowfish, pull him out," he commanded. "If he makes a sound," he tapped his sword, "cut out his tongue. Remember, we must save him for the boy."

"Yes, sir!"

The Morok was dragged out, his eyes bright with fear. Hands tightly bound, he was led away as two soldiers set about restoring the trap.

"There's a bag of something here, sir," one shouted. "Looks like powder. And some strange metal things."

Powder? Miago stepped forward. He knew that Moroks used poison; perhaps he could mix it with a fishing potion. "May

I have the powder, sir?"

The officer ignored him. "Throw it all away." He turned to Miago. "We've some questions for him," he said. "Then he's all yours. But not here. We must get back in the forest where it's safer."

The moon was high as they marched. The Morok limped and hopped as he struggled to keep up. When he slowed they struck him, when he groaned they laughed. Miago compared him with the soldiers and was surprised by his size. His dark hair was grey at the temples. Colourful bands adorned his neck and wrists. Weights pulled his ear lobes down and rings glinted on slim, elegant fingers. The swish of his soft clothing was in stark contrast with the harshness of Miago's tunic.

Miago turned to a soldier. "Just my luck I get to kill a scrawny one."

The soldier jabbed the Morok in the ribs, laughing when he yelped. "They're all like that!"

They marched hard for an hour before stopping. Miago was resting against a tree as the soldiers removed their helmets. "That's better," said one. "I can breathe again," Scar Neck added, fanning his sweating face with his hand. A ladder was retrieved from the undergrowth and one by one they climbed onto a small plateau. "Last man up bring the ladder," shouted the officer. The Morok was dragged to the rear of the plateau and thrown to the ground.

"Find out how many of them there are, where their camp is and if we were followed," the officer ordered.

Miago watched with mounting confusion as the Morok was interrogated. He knew that when they had their answers the man would be killed and that would be his job. Should he do it quickly and spare his suffering? But Moroks didn't feel pain so maybe he'd impress the soldiers and draw it out. But his thoughts were ripped apart by a terrible scream.

There was enjoyment in the soldier's voice, "Do you want me to burn you again, Morok? Now answer my questions!"

"This bit never takes long. Then it's your turn."

Miago spun around to face a soldier he didn't recognize. How could the man be so relaxed? Miago forced a weak smile but a second scream had him sitting bolt upright. "Don't worry about it," said the soldier. "He only looks human and he screams to fool us." He rubbed his hands. "Finally, it's my turn." Miago watched him hurry towards the slumped figure of the Morok.

Miago clamped his hands over his ears. When finally he removed them, he heard words above the whimpering.

"That's better! You see, even Moroks can be helpful."

Miago lost track of time but finally there was silence. Looking up, he saw the prone shape of the Morok. Had they killed him?

The officer was approaching.

"We have our information," he said. "When the rest of his people arrive, they will be ambushed and slaughtered. Now it's your turn." The man gave Miago a knife. "Recognise it? Now do to the Morok what you did to the shark."

The handle felt good and he liked the way the bone studs fitted between his fingers. He picked up a stone to sharpen it.

"Another thing – it's been agreed this kill will be added to your father's score. That'll make ten and will bring glory to your family."

Miago thought of his brother. "This is for you, Cufu," he whispered. "When all is said and done it's us or it's them."

He walked over to the Morok who was still slumped on the ground, his back exposed. At least I won't have to look him in the eye, Miago thought. In fact, it wouldn't be so difficult if he found the soft space between the ribs – much easier than killing the shark.

Miago knelt. Shallow breathing told him the man was still alive. He placed the blade on the Morok's back and the breathing stopped. He drew it carefully across his ribs, tracing each in turn. It was easy to count the bones because there was no fat on them. He stopped above the heart. The Morok tensed; he began whispering. Strange words poured from his mouth.

Was he praying? Miago tightened his grip and braced himself for the thrust. As he tensed his muscles, he laughed. It was only a Morok, after all.

The soldiers were dancing and singing. Miago saw how unsteady they'd become. He felt proud when they offered him a swig from a leather bottle but the liquid exploded in his throat and left him coughing and wheezing. The soldiers laughed; they said he was a good boy. One invited him to a party when they returned to the village; another said he knew a woman who'd make a man of him.

A soldier began to sing and everyone turned to watch him.

"If only I could sing like that," Miago said.

The singer caught Miago's eye. "Now it's the boy's turn to entertain us!" he shouted.

"Come on!" the others agreed.

"I can't sing," Miago stuttered. "Worst voice in the world!"

The officer came over. "I'll be the judge of that, now sing!" he said. "Do as I command!"

Miago felt his chest tighten. Fear would make his voice more strangled and, as he breathed deeply in preparation, he hated himself for being unable to sing. Why was it that, no matter how much he concentrated, he had no control over his voice? The officer was staring at him; the others waited. Perhaps closing his eyes would help. He summoned his courage and tried a note, struggling to control it. A second escaped but the laughter had already started.

"Voice like a frog!"

"That's an insult to frogs!"

A kinder voice joined in. "Don't worry about them, Miago."

In his embarrassment, Miago hadn't seen Blowfish approach.

"Leave the boy alone!" he growled. He gave Miago a bleary, drink-sodden smile. "You handled yourself pretty well in there."

Miago frowned. "In where?"

Blowfish gestured vaguely. "In front of the Supreme Council." He took a swig from a leather flask and offered it to Miago. "I was impressed and you know what?"

Miago sipped. "What?" he said, his eyes watering.

Blowfish leaned forward confidingly. "My daughter has a stuffed possum too. What did they say your brother's was called?"

"Bok Bok."

Miago watched as he started rubbing his face. It was as if he was trying to force out a thought. "Don't you think it's strange they knew its name?" he finally said.

Miago hesitated. "What do you mean?"

"The soldier who found it by the Morok camp knew its name," Blowfish mumbled. "But if the Moroks took your brother, and the soldiers followed them … and your brother dropped the possum …" He paused and considered his conclusion. "How could one of them have heard its name without talking to your brother? But they never found him. Doesn't make sense …" On unsteady legs Blowfish staggered away. "Anyway, I'm not paid to think."

Miago studied Blowfish carefully and thought about what he'd said. He was right – it didn't seem to make sense. And Blowfish, he decided, you're not as stupid as you look.

Miago knew he should join the celebrations so he walked over and asked for a drink. They didn't notice how little he took, how he swilled it around his mouth, turned and spat it out.

"The thing I like abou' you, boy, ish your imaginashun." The soldier was swaying. "Fire ant mound! Who woulda thorta that?" He belched. "Ruined our fun, you did, till I thought about it!"

Miago was careful to sway as he spoke. "It's no fun killing him with a knife, over too quickly. The Morok's half dead already but if we tied him to the ant mound, everyone can watch him get eaten alive."

"Anyone ever tell you, you gotta mean streak?" the soldier said approvingly. "You'd make a good solja!" Slowly the man slid down to settle on his knees. He closed his eyes and his head flopped to one side.

"Sleep well," Miago whispered.

Miago laughed with the other soldiers, taking care that they saw him drinking but when they weren't looking he continued to spit it out. He stumbled over to the officer. "Sir, everything's spinning and I feel a bit –" He collapsed and crawled a short distance. He dragged himself up, then fell heavily.

"I think that's enough dizzy juice for him," the officer laughed.

Miago rolled over and closed his eyes but sleep didn't come. He had enjoyed the party and some of the soldiers even seemed to like him. He smiled at his idea of tying the Morok to the fire ant mound but Blowfish's words kept returning and they still made no sense. Perhaps the Morok knew something about it. Miago listened and waited. Soon the singing was replaced by snoring. Carefully he looked around. The moonlight revealed the soldiers who slept where they'd dropped. Silently he crawled towards the Morok.

"I know you can't understand me, Morok, but just because I didn't kill you doesn't mean … "

The man turned slowly. Miago saw a face etched with pain, wet with tears. "How you think soldiers speak with me?"

"But –"

"I know some of your language."

"You do?"

"As children we must learn other tongues."

Miago frowned. "Hard Hands said the same thing but I thought Moroks only grunted."

The Morok looked down. "I wish you already kill me, boy," he said, crushed. "Why you want torture me on fire ant mound?" When he got no answer, he said, "I watching you. Why you make soldiers think you drunk? Why you pretend sleep?"

"Because I hadn't made my mind up about you, Morok."

The Morok shook his head. "You call me Morok … this is word of insult invented by your people. We call ourselves Quma and we proud of who we are."

The conversation wasn't going as Miago had planned. "Well, Morok or Quma, whatever you call yourself," he said, trying to

regain the upper ground, "you are a murdering, cruel, uncivilized people. You come each year to kill, to steal, to poison us. We must protect ourselves."

"What your name is, boy?"

"None of your business."

"I prefer use name than call you boy."

"It's … Miago," he finally said. "And your name's still Morok!"

The man started coughing and he tried to muffle the noise with his hands. Miago saw the blood in his palms.

"You're …"

His eyes were dark. "I bleed inside."

Miago shifted uncomfortably. "I have to hate you, Morok," he said, almost pleadingly. "Our people have always been at war."

"That no true."

"Yes, it is," Miago insisted. "Even when the volcano erupted, you Moroks stole into our city to steal and murder."

The man shook his head. "No. We send people to help. We friends then, but our men ambushed by your people, the ones in black."

"You would say that!"

"We no murderers, Miago," he continued. "We pass here every year and must stop to rest and feed cattle but you always attack and kill us."

Miago was pale with anger. "But you took my brother! Was he murdered and eaten? Or was he worked to death as a slave?"

The Quma looked shocked. "What you talk about? We no take children!"

"You only deny it because we've caught you," Miago hissed.

"If he taken, he taken by someone else."

Miago couldn't believe what he was hearing. "Other children disappear too and it only happens when you Moroks arrive. Explain that!"

"I sorry about children but not my people who take them."

"So what were you doing on our hill?"

"*Your* hill?" The Quma laughed weakly. "Is only hill."

"Don't anger me, Morok."

The Quma's voice softened. "I come look. I hide in forest and watch your people. If I liked what I see, I come into village ..."

"To murder and steal!" Miago interrupted triumphantly.

The Quma shook his head. "To meet as friend."

"You're only saying this so that I don't kill you."

"I had bag medicine powder and metal fish hooks. They gift but soldier throw away."

"*Metal* fish hooks?" Miago studied him. Was he lying? "The powder was poison!"

The Quma lifted his bound arms. "Pull back sleeve."

Miago felt the softness of the fabric. Beneath it was a bracelet of entwined gold, bronze and iron. "Eel, snake, worm," the man explained.

"Does it mean something?"

"Snake live with belly on ground. Snake mean life but he close to soil where dead are buried to remind us death never far away. Worm live in soil who eat us when we buried. Eel in ocean, where spirit goes when dead. As ocean has no end, eel mean afterlife."

"What strange beliefs you have!"

"Only sound strange to you, Miago. Your people no make jewellery like this or fine clothes," he said. "Our people best metalworkers ... we make finest rings, swords, arrow heads, cooking pots ... you think barbarians make these things?"

Miago didn't answer.

"We have other things your people need. We can even get rain fever cure."

"A cure?"

"Yes. We buy from distant people. It come from bark of tree that grow on mountains much higher than volcano."

Miago laughed. "Taller than our volcano?"

"Ten of your volcanoes no reach top of their mountains."

"I've heard mountains are cold places," said Miago. "What does cold feel like?"

"I no been there but those people never cold because have animal that make warmest clothing. Animal has long neck and spit when angry."

"What are the people like?"

The Quma shrugged. "They worship giant vulture. They must keep bird happy or it pick up goat and flies into clouds. Then it drop goat on house!"

"A bird does *that*?"

Instead of answering, the man groaned. Miago leaned forward. "Are you all right?" he asked, confused. "I thought you couldn't feel pain."

The Quma breathed out. "You say many strange things."

Miago was silent.

"Let me tell you story," the Quma said. "When I finish, if you no believe me, then you kill me. Promise you no tie me on ant mound?"

Miago looked around nervously. "Will it take long?"

He began slowly. "Every spring Quma have contest to see who best fighter. When man win, family honoured. He then marry most beautiful of our women, he given more cows, faster horse, bigger tent.

"Every year I enter contest because I want these things. But I no win. One year I train all winter and I lift rocks to make body strong and run with hunting dogs so no get tired.

"I faced younger man. Fight start under sun, finish under stars. I tried all I know but he always had answer. Then he choke me but I no stop fighting. Last I remember crowd shouting at me to give up. They threw water in face to wake me. Man who won standing over me, laughing. I still hear that laugh when I sleep."

"And?"

The Quma sighed. "Recently I came to know truth."

"How did that happen?"

"I dare think about things I no think about before. One day I walk through forest. I sit on beach and watch parrots, young turtles. I look at water. I see things in air and water at same time."

"I don't understand."

"Is difficult explain. I see same things above water and upside down in water."

"You mean things reflected?"

"Yes. It make me think things not always as they seem. Me think about who I am. Not who I pretend to be to make others happy. I understand something important ..."

"What?"

"Yes, I hated man who beat me. But ... I hated me most of all.

"You hated yourself?"

"And hate one thing I could do as well as any man. So I hated foreigners. That easy because I no look them in eye, no speak with them, no see them working, thinking, laughing ... loving. And when I hate them it feel good. I became warrior, I kill men, some your people."

"You killed my people, Morok?" said Miago, horrified. "You were foolish to tell me!"

The Quma ignored him. "But recently I change. I woke up from sleep. I realized killing must hurt you like it hurt us. So I come meet your people as friend. That why I bring gifts."

"If what you say is true then you are a brave man." said Miago. He thought about everything he had been taught. "You are so ... different from what I expected." He held that thought as he asked, "You said you have a wife. Do you have children?"

The moonlight flashed on the tears in the Quma's eyes. "No wife, no children now."

Miago pulled out his knife. The Quma saw it and recoiled. "So, so you kill me?" he paused, "with Quma knife?"

Miago froze. "Quma knife?"

The man nodded. "Look at pattern in metal. Only Quma make knife like that. Look – our sacred symbol, head of bull."

"I wondered what that animal was."

"Are scratches on handle?"

Miago didn't need to look. "Yes. Why?"

"That ceremonial knife. One mark for each person. How you get knife?"

This was a very strange conversation, Miago thought. "From a man called Monkey Blood."

"Monkey Blood? You give people name like *that*?"

Miago shrugged. He raised the knife. The Quma gasped and

closed his eyes.

"Kill me quick. I no scream. Will end pain."

"It's all right," Miago soothed, cutting the straps that bound him before helping him stand. "Can you walk?"

The Quma put his arm around Miago's shoulders. Carefully they made their way to the edge of the camp and to the rock face where Miago lowered the ladder.

"Go quickly before someone sees us."

Instead the Quma knelt to pray.

Miago glanced back at the sleeping soldiers. "You don't have time for that," he whispered.

Finally the Quma stood. He embraced Miago. "I no forget you."

"Good luck!" Miago said.

The Quma stepped onto the ladder. When he reached the bottom, he looked up. "Maybe we meet again? You and me teach our people to be friends?"

"I hope so," Miago said quietly. "Goodbye ... Quma."

The man was disappearing into the forest as Miago pulled up the ladder. His parting words made Miago smile. "No pull up ladder or they know someone help me escape."

There was more.

"Miago, I pray one day all men discover *tocamu*."

Tocamu? Miago sighed deeply. Who was the Chameleon, this soft-spoken man with the power to change how people thought? Had he also used riddles on this Quma who seemed to have rejected the teachings of his own people? Miago felt an urge to climb down the ladder and go after him but he knew it was too dangerous, and, though his eyes searched the blackness of the night, the Quma was gone.

Back among the soldiers, it didn't take Miago long to find what he needed. He picked up a flask and held it to his lips. Coughing and spluttering, he forced himself to drink. He felt the heat in his throat and soon the dizziness came. He went back to where he had been lying and settled down again.

It was mid-morning when Miago heard the shouting. He opened his eyes and a bolt of pain exploded in his brain. Soldiers were running back and forth.

"He's escaped, the Morok's gone!"

The officer was shouting orders. "Break camp. Mongoose, take Blowfish with you and don't come back without that Morok!" He looked across at Miago. "Someone help the boy up," he said. "And tell him the fire ants will have to wait."

BE BRAVE MY BROTHER

The day before the ceremony dawned warm and still. Miago had slept fitfully and he rose early. To keep himself busy he combed the forest for something to sell but he found it difficult to concentrate because a fear was nagging at him: tonight he must sleep in the forest.

T'lu-i was at the new stall, stomping around and obviously angry. "I've sold some pretty stones and all my coral but when I think of the tribute we pay Banakaloo-Piki, I've made no profit. Daddy's black gold had better make money."

"Do you know what it is yet?" he asked.

T'lu-i held up her hands. Her fingers were black. "This happened when I cleaned out the cart. Whatever it is, it doesn't wash off."

"The answer could be in the temple," Miago suggested.

"Why do you say that?"

"I'm not sure yet. When I am, I'll tell you."

"Tell me or I'll …" With a giggle, T'lu-i moved towards him.

"Don't," Miago said firmly. She frowned in surprise but he didn't feel like playing games. "We need to talk but not here. Meet me by the well as soon as you can leave the stall."

Miago killed time by dropping pebbles down the well. He debated whether or not to tell T'lu-i about the cargo her father had delivered to the temple and the knives he sold behind her back. But would she believe him? Looking up, he saw her approaching and he admired the half-dance in her step. He felt a tingle of dizziness as her taut body flexed under the loose fabric

and he glanced around before whispering, "What a vision *that* would be!"

"Are you all right, Miago?"

Miago felt proud that she had come. She even looked a little nervous in front of him. He reached out his hand. "Oh, T'lu-i, I've worried so much about my Life Choice. I still can't decide."

She sighed. "Maybe you should seek guidance."

"You mean the Moon Swing?"

"Yes."

"They can tie their symbols to it and drape offerings in the trees but that old swing never talks. It's only the surf on the beach – it makes noises because the sand's different there."

"Granna swore you can hear words if you know how to listen."

"Your grandmother also said she could tell the future by watching birds." His voice took on a mocking tone. "That an old storm eagle guided her. Hah!"

"It's true. She'd ask it questions and if it circled one way, that meant 'yes', the other way meant 'no'. When Granna died her spirit entered the bird and it flew away. I never saw it again."

"Oh, T'lu-i! You sit on the swing if you want."

"She said you had the gift Miago but you wouldn't use it."

"T'lu-i, we need to talk about more important things."

"There are too many people here," she said, glancing around. "Let's walk."

They left the village and climbed a lava flow on a path that skirted the vegetable plots. Parrots screeched overhead as the track twisted through the lower forest. They came to a dry river bed spanned by a stone bridge.

"There's never water here. So why build this bridge?" Miago asked.

"I've wondered that myself," T'lu-i replied, leaning her head on Miago's shoulder. "But sometimes, when it's very still, you can hear trickling water."

"You don't need a bridge for a trickle!"

T'lu-i pointed. "Look at the size of those stones. They're round – that means they were moved by water."

"Maybe the river changed course in the forest," Miago suggested.

"We could ask *them*."

A man and woman were approaching; the mark of the Believer showed clearly on their foreheads.

Miago stepped forward and addressed the man. "Excuse me, Iron Feather. Do you know why there's a bridge here when there's no water?"

"And such a strong one," T'lu-i added.

"Young man, we don't trouble ourselves with such matters,"

replied the man. "But it must exist to serve the wishes of our Great Goddess."

"And it's not our right to question her wishes," the woman added solemnly.

"Thank you for being so helpful," Miago muttered as they passed from sight.

T'lu-i giggled. "You're so disrespectful!"

They walked in silence towards the bay where the forest's shadow gave way to brilliant sunlight. Standing on the edge of the beach, they let their eyes adjust. A tumbled mass of boulders linked the forest and beach and upon it a troop of monkeys jumped and chattered.

"I've given them names," T'lu-i said, pointing. "See that one with the short tail? He's called Digger because he likes to ..." The monkey was lifting stones, his hands scattering the sand. "And that one's Pirate. He steals from the others. And there's Peacock." She laughed. "Watch. She likes to flirt with the boys."

"But Peacock's a boy's name!"

Peacock moved towards a young monkey that sat beyond the group. She preened herself before moving closer to him but he walked away.

"She's not very good at it!" T'lu-i grinned. "But that one is shy."

"What's his name?" asked Miago.

T'lu-i fidgeted.

"Yes?"

"I call him … Miago."

"Am I that bad?" he asked in surprise.

"Come on!" T'lu-i said. They stepped onto the sand and the monkeys turned to watch them before slipping back into the forest. "I leave food for them but they always run away," she explained. "One day maybe they'll trust me."

Miago joined her in the shade of a boulder, their backs pressed against the warm stone. T'lu-i raised a hand. "Look, fresh turtle tracks. And there's a new nest. Fifty days from now I'll be here to help them get to the surf."

When Miago didn't speak, T'lu-i turned to face him. "I know you didn't come here to talk about turtles, Miago. There's something you need to know. I've made my Life Choice," she said softly. "I've spoken to my father. I trust his advice."

Miago was indignant. "But you take his advice because he tells you what you want to hear. What about what you *need*?"

T'lu-i shook her head. "Oh, Miago, stop torturing yourself. What I want and need are the same thing. I take his advice because he understands me. You suffer because you insist on questioning everything." She took Miago's hand, her fingers kneading his palm. "You think too much. Why can't you be like everyone else?"

"Because I'm not like everyone else."

She hesitated. "Why do you say that?"

He looked down. "When I was younger, I used to have visions. They stopped when Cufu died."

"So Granna was right."

"My family told me not to speak about it but the visions have started again. I had one the other day when I was swimming. I was in the city before the volcano erupted."

She was studying him closely now. "Tell me what it was like."

"Incredibly beautiful and full of … love. Yet I felt …" he paused while he searched for the right words, "I didn't deserve to be there."

"Go on."

"Another thing." Miago spoke slowly. "Do you ever feel there's someone standing behind you but when you turn round, no one's there?"

"Granna used to talk about something like that. She called it her visitor. She said when I was old enough, she'd explain but she died." T'lu-i squeezed his hand, her tone changing. "May I say something?"

"Depends."

"Father says you changed when you lost Cufu," she said gently. "He says you were very close."

Miago was silent.

"I know you'll always miss him, but you mustn't blame the whole world for what happened."

The lump in his throat stopped Miago from speaking.

"Miago, we are lucky. We have our Men of Knowledge and our Goddess who protects us." She pulled his hand until he looked up. "I know life's not perfect but it could be much worse. Miago, say something."

"If our Men of Knowledge and the Goddess are so good and so powerful, why do they allow all the suffering?" Miago snatched his hand away. "Give me an example of when they've done some good."

"You told me that when Rain Dancer was sick, a Man of Knowledge sent a healer who saved her," T'lu-i said triumphantly.

"But we had to sell things to pay him and there's a potion that works better."

T'lu-i shook her head. "People always say that."

"It's true! It comes from the bark of a tree that grows on distant mountains where long-necked animals spit and birds drop goats on houses."

T'lu-i burst out laughing. "Miago, *who* have you been talking to?"

He ignored her question. "How can I believe in the Men of Knowledge when I see so much suffering?"

"Suffering's part of life," T'lu-i insisted. "You just have to accept it."

Miago jumped to his feet. "Well, I don't!" he shouted. He paced the beach, kicking the sand. He picked up a stone and hurled it against the boulders. "Monkeys!" he called in desperation. "How do you feel about life? Do you suffer all day long?"

"Miago I've never heard you talk like this," T'lu-i said, visibly upset. "It's because of him, isn't it? He's put ideas into your head."

"The Chameleon?"

"I thought we called him the Maker?"

"He changed his name."

"Why?"

"Never mind."

"Are you still talking to him?" she said fearfully, her voice rising. "Miago, he's a stranger, you don't know anything about him. You talk to him and suddenly everything you've learned is forgotten. Why, Miago, what's so special about him?"

"Firstly, I trust him."

"You *trust* him?"

"And he's ... my friend." Miago blushed as he said it.

"Your *friend*?" she said in amazement. "Miago, I'm your friend. Your family are your friends. The people you grew up with are your friends but this man ..."

Miago spoke quietly. "You don't trust him."

"Why should I?" She watched him push the sand with his toes. "I've decided to be a Worker," she said softly. "You proved yourself worthy by killing that shark and I heard you did well on patrol and, and Daddy likes you and he will teach you how to make money. That's what you want, isn't it?"

He shrugged.

"If you become a Worker and if you still want me ..."

Miago saw how wide her eyes had become.

" ... then I want you for my husband." Confused by Miago's silence, she continued. "We could live and work together. You could carry on diving, I'll sell what you catch. Miago?"

With a sigh he sat down and took her hand again. "At least you don't bite your nails like me."

She squeezed his hand but he didn't respond. "Miago, what's

wrong? Please tell me!"

He was watching a seabird as it skimmed the waves. "I've dreamed of this moment," he said finally. "But as my dream comes true, I feel doubt. I'm pulled one way by my love for you and my love of the sea, but another by the laws of this place."

T'lu-i began to cry.

"I don't know if I can make the choice they demand of me," Miago said desperately. "If it means losing you, that may be the price I'll pay."

"Miago?"

After a pause he said, "But, T'lu-i, it doesn't have to be like this!"

She pulled away from him. "You can't mean ... the caves?"

"Come with me!" he begged. "Together we'll be twice as strong!"

"You're mad! We'll both be killed. Many people don't even get past the Guardians. Remember the Red Orchids! There were ten of them ..."

"But we could work as a team." he said, full of passion now. "And with what I've learned from the Chameleon ..."

"You know there's no escape! Anyway, I can't risk it because of Daddy. He'll need me when he's old."

"He can afford to pay someone to look after him," Miago muttered.

"I promised my mother when she was dying," T'lu-i said, anger and frustration in her voice. "I'll make you happy. Let me, Miago! Don't ask me to risk the caves; don't take the challenge yourself ... *Please!*"

"It depends on whether I survive tonight," he pointed out.

"Where will you sleep?"

"You know I can't tell you but Hard Hands helped me choose somewhere that looks safe."

"Promise you'll be careful?"

"I promise."

T'lu-i was rubbing her tear-stained face. "I've wished we'd be free one day," she whispered. "I dreamed we were dolphins playing in the warm ocean, jumping, chasing flying fish ..." her voice tailed off.

Miago drew her closer. T'lu-i's soft hair caressed his cheek and she pressed herself against him. She was quiet now but he noticed how deeply she breathed. Struggling with his thoughts, Miago brushed the hair from her face and kissed her gently on the forehead. Her eyes held his and he saw a fear and uncertainty that she'd always hidden so well. He stayed that way, a prisoner to her warmth and the scent of flowers.

Finally he spoke. "Oh, T'lu-i, I promise it'll work out for the best. Don't ask me how ... but I know it will."

"No, Miago, you *hope* it will and that's different." She pushed him away and her head dropped into her hands. He watched her but he could think of nothing to say so, to the sounds of her sobbing, he walked slowly away.

It was late afternoon and Miago was surveying the place with care. On three sides the vegetation was tangled and thick and his confidence grew when he saw the puncture vine that wove through it; ahead, the ground was level and dry. Dropping on all fours he studied the ground in search of animal tracks. He saw the delicate impressions left by coconut rats, the tracks of a monitor lizard and the spoor of a dwarf antelope.

Miago looked for more clues such as broken twigs and flattened grasses. Where he found stones, he turned them to check for dampness. He was relieved to see that the foliage wasn't dense enough to conceal a man and that the overhead branches were too thin to support a large animal. He worked hard, keeping his mind busy because a gnawing terror seemed determined to consume him with images and sounds of the night.

A tree grew in the centre of the clearing and where the trunk met the forest floor he found a hole. Curious, Miago tapped the entrance with his knife. What leapt out was covered in hair and was as big as Miago's hand. The eyes were red, the mouthparts wet. It sprang on the knife, wrapping its legs around the blade as a fist closes on a stone. Miago heard the tapping of fang on metal. Revolted, he flung the knife down and the rat spider scurried back into its lair.

Miago prodded the hole again. This time there was no response. I should have hacked it to pieces and left it for the ants, he thought. Now it might return in the night to bite him.

Miago walked to the back of the clearing and he started work on an escape route by cutting a path through the vegetation. He collected some branches, trimming both ends into sharp points before forcing them into the ground, their shafts angled away from him. Some he set low, others at waist height; a few were level with his head. Miago repeated Damago's words to himself:

you can stroke a porcupine from its head to its tail but you can't stroke it from its tail to its head. He was perspiring heavily now and a buzzing warned him the sweat bees had found him. Miago had brought a munjo fruit and he rubbed it onto his skin, throwing pieces around his sleeping area. He strung up the hammock and lined it with palm leaves. Glancing back at the open ground he said, "If I'd spent less time with T'lu-i I could have protected my front with a spring trap."

He pulled Bok Bok from his tunic. "You'll look after me,

won't you?" He saw the torn ear, the holes. "Cufu, I promise I'll mend him if you protect me tonight." He took out a package and opened it carefully to reveal the damp moss inside. He wiped the knife blade on the moss and held it up to dry, before laying the knife on the ground beside him. He covered the blade with stones and climbed into the hammock before pulling a rough blanket over himself. His instinct was to cower, to curl into a shivering ball and await his fate but a feeling had started and he let it come. It drifted into his mind and took the form of words: *be brave, my brother.* But no sooner had he heard it than it was gone. He lifted the blanket to confirm that he was alone. I'll try, Cufu, he thought. Then, keeping his promise, Miago drew a deep breath and addressed the forest.

"The blade is coated in toad sweat. If anything touches it, it will die. So, creatures of the jungle, you have been warned!" The light was gone now and Miago was alone with his fears and prayers. He lay listening to the unfamiliar noises, aware that his knowledge of the daytime forest was of no use now.

The dream started with a soft light. The shapes and colours told Miago it was the city of his ancestors with its great palace and pink temple. This time Miago felt contentment and a sense of belonging; when he looked at the people, he admired their serenity. They were elegant in their dress and conduct. As he walked among them, the women nodded in greeting and the men stood aside to let him pass.

Everything was ordered and clean. Miago walked across an open square where people mingled with marble statues. He came to a well where laughing girls drew buckets of crystal-clear water. He accepted a drink from one and a smile from another as the sound of laughter drifted over to him.

Beyond the well sat a group of children. Miago saw that they surrounded a board covered with squares that was decorated with pictures of the sea. Approaching them he saw a girl push a large wooden fish across the board. A boy then placed a smaller one beside it. "True or false?" he asked. In the centre of the board lay a wooden chest with a tortoiseshell lid. It rested on a square of purple silk that was decorated with gold thread. Miago moved closer.

"What's in the box?" he asked the children.

He didn't wait for an answer because he'd recognized one of them. "Cufu!" he gasped. "I thought you were … d–"

As Miago stared, he found himself accepting the situation because it somehow felt normal. He looked at the game again. "What's the name of the game?"

"We call it Jack's Dilemma," a boy answered.

"Who's Jack?"

"Jack's not a person. There's a type of fish called a jack."

Miago nodded. "What's its dilemma?"

Cufu spoke. "When he in ocean, worms grow on scales, in mouth and gills."

"So?"

"When he come to reef, small fish swim up from coral. It eat

157

worms. Make him clean and he no itch no more."

Miago knew all this. "We call them cleaner fish."

"Then jack open mouth and cleaner swim inside. He eat worms there too. It do same in gills." Cufu continued. "But there's big dir ... dirl-"

"Dilemma?" Miago prompted.

"Yes! What if jack hungry?"

Miago thought he understood. "You mean why doesn't he swallow the cleaner fish?"

"Jack no eat cleaner fish because ..." Cufu looked around for help and an older girl took over.

"It gets cleaned for free and the cleaner fish gets an easy meal. Both are happy because they solve the other's problem. If the jacks ate the cleaner fish, then word would spread and they wouldn't come to clean him or his friends."

"I see," said Miago.

Another boy joined in. "But there's another fish, he looks like a cleaner fish and he behaves like one too. The jack lets him swim into its gills but he has sharp teeth. Instead of eating the worms he takes a bite out of the jack."

Miago considered this. "So the jack has two dilemmas. Whether or not to eat the cleaner fish and to guess if the fish he let into his gills is the real thing."

The girl was talking again. "If one jack ate the cleaners he'd get cleaned and he'd get a free meal. If a few of them did that the cleaner fish would stop coming."

"Are you saying the jacks never eat the cleaner fish?" Miago pressed.

An older boy spoke. "Never. The jacks and the cleaner fish signed a treaty. Even though the false cleaners take advantage, it's the best way overall. So the jacks put up with some bites from the false cleaners so that their deal with the real cleaners survives."

"But a jack that ate cleaners now and then would get the best of both worlds," Miago pointed out. So it's best to be a cheating jack or a fake cleaner."

Cufu sounded serious. "That how most *people* behave! Game

teach me if I behave like that, soon no one happy." Cufu smiled at his brother, "Game teach Miago about trust."

A memory was playing on Miago's mind. Hadn't the Chameleon said something about fish knowing more about trust than people?

A message from the waking world had begun to invade Miago's dream. He pushed it away, longing to stay with Cufu who was speaking, "… then the winner opens chest."

"What's inside it?"

"You must earn right to open box, Miago," Cufu said.

"Earn the right?"

The dream was becoming blurred and Cufu's voice grew distant. Miago fought as he tried to concentrate on the children but it didn't help. "Let me stay with you!" he pleaded, desperate to stay in the dream.

But now there was something moving that crouched on the very edge of his mind. Miago tensed, gripped by a wave of fear as cold fingers reached from the waking world and shook him.

Were they part of the dream? Miago's heart was pounding. Slowly he pulled the blanket off his head but the night was as dark as pitch. Was someone out there listening? Waiting?

He heard a noise like something heavy pressing on dried leaves. Footsteps? He slipped from the hammock and reached for the knife. Edging forward, keeping low, he held the knife out to impale an attacker. Ahead a twig snapped. Was that breathing? Then the clouds parted and the clearing was flooded with moonlight.

In a second he had searched left and right but he saw nothing. But when he looked at the trunk of the tree there was a movement: a body and legs – he imagined the red eyes and revolting mouth. The spider raised itself and began to pulse gently as it prepared to strike. Miago leapt back. Rat spiders jumped.

Something was wrong – the spider was hairless. As a fresh wave of fear swept through him, he realized that the spider was a hand and the shadow a man, crouching behind the tree. A Morok!

Miago stepped forward but in that instant a cloud covered

the moon, plunging the clearing into darkness. He thrust with the knife but the blade struck bark. Panicking, he struck again, but then something leapt on him from the side, knocking the knife away, and they fell in a tangle of limbs. Where he'd expected cropped, matted hair, he was tickled by curls. Instead of a bitter stench, he smelt flowers and the attacking scream was no scream at all; more a gasp of surprise. The gasp turned into a word: "Miago!"

"T-T'lu-i!" he gulped. "I nearly killed you!"

She was lying on him and she made no effort to move. Instead she pressed her hand over his mouth. "Sssshhhh!" she hissed. "Don't make so much noise."

Miago dragged her fingers away and lowered his voice. "If I'd even cut you ..."

He had touched her before but never like this. All he could see was the outline of her face. All he could feel was her.

Confused, Miago tried to roll her off but she locked him there, pinning him with her arms and legs. "I didn't know you were so strong!" he gulped. Or that he was so weak.

Her lips brushed his ear. Her breathing was heavy and he felt the rise and fall of her chest.

"Miago, I *had* to see you! The way you left me ... I've been going out of my mind!"

"T'lu-i, what if someone finds us? They'll think we're –"

"I don't care."

"But you know the law. It's too dangerous." Miago fought his feelings and tried to push her off. "If someone finds out you came here ... How did you find me?"

"I bribed Hard Hands!"

Slowly the clouds parted and the clearing was bathed in a milky light. T'lu-i's voice was breathless. "Miago, we may never get another chance."

Miago fought to control himself. He tried to sound angry. "It isn't allowed, if we get caught –"

"I don't care! Who knows what will happen after tomorrow?"

She stayed where she was, pressing down on him, her

breathing short and deep. He lay there in his ecstasy and panic and he didn't know if he could fight her.

"But –"

"Sssshhhh."

He held T'lu-i as he marvelled at the softness of her skin, the warmth of her body as one part of their destiny became clear.

But a message was seeping into his mind: *you know this is wrong.* Miago tried to ignore it, concentrating on T'lu-i, but it grew louder. He cursed. Why must he ruin everything? He thought about the other boys – none of them would resist her. He was so lucky she had chosen him but he loathed himself because he knew he must stop.

"T'lu-i, oh T'lu-i," he whispered, his voice cracking, holding her wrists as he tried to explain. "It will happen. One day we will be together but not here. Not now."

His hand cupped the back of her head and he pulled her close. For minutes there was silence; then Miago felt her tears.

"Miago!" she sobbed. "You don't want me!"

"T'lu-i, believe me, I do," he said fervently. "Every second I dream of you but something's wrong."

"Something's wrong! *What's* wrong?"

"I don't know!" He shook his head in frustration. "Just a voice in my head, I suppose. And, and I'm so sorry but I had to obey ... T'lu-i?"

She propped herself on her elbows and studied him. "That's strange."

"What?

"Before I came here, I went to the Moon Swing and I asked for guidance. I asked what you must do."

"And?"

"Miago, I heard words. I swear it. I didn't know whether to tell you."

"It was your imagination."

"No, no, it wasn't. They repeated again and again: Miago must *listen and obey.*"

"It was just the waves on the sand. And who should I obey? My parents, the Men of Knowledge, the Chameleon, Monkey

Blood ... you?"

"Oh, Miago ... I wish I knew."

They lay in the moonlight's changing shadows until they turned to watch a speck of light that rose flashing to circle above them. It was joined by others. Soon dozens, then hundreds, of tiny beacons were drawn to an invisible centre that pulsed and heaved in a maelstrom of cool light. When the mating dance ended, the fireflies melted back into the night. Miago and T'lu-i struggled with shared thoughts. She closed her eyes and whispered, "It's so much easier for them."

In their stillness they didn't feel the dampness that settled with the mist or hear the distant animal calls that broke the silence.

Miago was drifting off when she whispered, "I must get back." She kissed him softly, "And you must sleep."

"The moon is still up so go quickly and keep to the path," he warned her.

"I will."

"Don't stop for anything."

Miago sighed as she slipped away. He climbed back into the hammock, and glanced around before pulling the blanket over his head. He listened and he thought, but soon he was overcome by a wretched loneliness that was unlike anything he'd known. He lay there sobbing as his misery grew until he forgot about the Moroks and the animals of the night.

THE SUPREME RULER

When morning came, Miago climbed wearily from the hammock. He yawned as he wondered how somewhere so tranquil at dawn could hold such terror at night. A bird sang overhead. Miago thought he knew all the forest's birdsongs but this was different. He looked up to see a small bird. "If you are saying good morning, and wishing me a good day, then I'll wish you the same. But, you know what? This could be the worst day of my life." He untied the hammock and retrieved the knife though his thoughts were of T'lu-i. The previous night felt like a lifetime ago. Why had he ruined it? Why had he rejected her? *You fool, Miago! You probably won't get another chance …*

He was about to leave when he saw figures approaching. They were some way off but four of them were unmistakeable: they were Men of Knowledge. The fifth, however, was very different. Miago could see the animal skin draped over a purple tunic and how the morning sunlight flashed on gold thread. What a strange but important looking man, Miago thought – he must be something to do with the ceremony but Miago didn't feel like meeting anyone so he ducked behind a bush. He waited but they didn't come. Finally he stood and looked around but no one was there.

The bird had stopped singing now and, when he glanced up, it had flown. He started for the village. When he emerged from the forest he saw that the road to the square was lined with torches and bunches of flowers. He knew that the women had washed their finest clothes and would bully their men into bathing. The dogs would be let loose in the forest to ward off evil spirits, and the babies would be given a sleeping draught.

It was a day of fasting but food was the last thing on Miago's mind. Home now, he was pacing his room as he listened to his parents arguing.

He had never heard this tone from his mother. "He survived the night in the forest so he's earned the right to know! I *will* tell him! If you don't want to hear it, you can leave." For a moment there was silence and Miago tried to imagine the look on his father's face. His mother shouted, "Mudskipper, please come in!"

Miago entered and glanced at his parents in turn. Rain Dancer sat in silence while Thunder Fly stared at the floor. Silver Rain's voice was level. "Mudskipper, what you need to know is that some people say there was a Supreme Ruler who lived in a great palace far away. He ruled our ancestors and many other peoples."

"Did he rule the Moroks?"

"They say he ruled everyone. But the Supreme Ruler, unlike our Men of Knowledge, didn't impose his will on his peoples – he let them make their own choices, and, over time, some developed into warring nations, others became ungodly."

"Stop, woman!" Thunder Fly protested weakly. "You'll only add to the boy's confusion!"

Silver Rain glared at her husband. "There were those who lived only for the physical pleasures of life; others who despised people because their skin colour, customs or spiritual beliefs were different. There were rich men who'd do anything to get richer but never worried about the suffering their greed caused. Others destroyed the land by killing too much game, or wounded the oceans with poison."

"You mean how Six Toes fishes is *wrong*?"

"Miago, the Befores never used poison."

"But they took many fish!"

"There were times when the ocean was so alive with fish that their nets made no difference. But in the bad years they always removed them." She continued, "Returning to the story, there were men who sought the power to rule but abused it ... even people who interpreted the wisdom of the gods to suit their evil intentions. So the Supreme Ruler despaired. But one people developed in a way that did please him."

Thunder Fly had heard enough. He stormed out, cursing.

"But there were two problems. One was that some of the Supreme Ruler's courtiers were evil, and they plotted to take

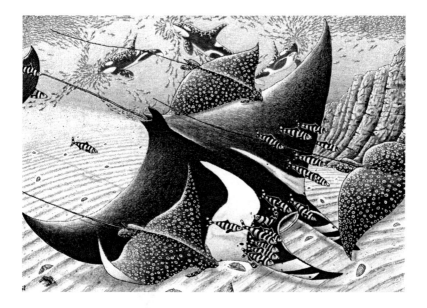

control of his kingdom."

"And the second?" Miago pressed.

She spoke slowly. "The people that pleased him ..."

"Yes?"

"They lived under the shadow of a great volcano."

Miago's mouth fell open. "You mean ...?"

Silver Rain nodded. "The Supreme Ruler had a son and it was decided he would come here to meet the Befores to help preserve their beliefs."

They were interrupted by a cough. Thunder Fly entered slowly. His smile looked forced. "Will you have me back?"

Miago sighed. "You should be with us, Father."

"Well if you *must* hear this, you should hear it from both of us," he said. He cleared his throat. "The evil courtiers attacked and there was a great battle. There was real danger that the evil ones would triumph but at last the battle was won and they were banished to the remotest part of the jungle. Then the Supreme Ruler's son came here. They say he was dressed in the most exquisite clothing – he arrived wearing a bird-shaped crown, a jungle cat skin was thrown over his shoulders. Shells decorated his belt, and beautiful feathers were woven into a tunic of purple and gold."

"Wait!" shouted Miago, "The man you describe ..."

"Yes?"

"I saw him this morning!"

They spoke in unison: "You *saw* him?"

"In the forest, surrounded by Men of Knowledge." He remembered the singing bird and the bright colours. "I saw a strange little bird too. It was brown and yellow ... with a crest on its head."

"That sounds like a painted lady. But they were wiped out by the volcano."

"So it was another vision."

Silver Rain sighed. "I thought they had stopped, Mudskipper."

"We have little time. It's important we finish the story,"

Thunder Fly interrupted.

"Please continue, Father."

"He met the elders and they spoke about how their beliefs could be preserved. At first, they discussed saving this knowledge with the spoken word but they knew how badly speech survives the passage of time. Then they thought of writing it down but there were problems with that too."

"That many people can't read?"

"Yes. Though this wisdom applied to all, it would not be understood by those who spoke other tongues."

"So what did they do?"

"The Supreme Ruler's son realized he must design a symbol that could be understood by all people for all time. He fashioned it from metal and showed it to the elders."

"What did it look like?"

"No one knows. They say it revealed the secret of how man can live in peace with himself, his own people and even with strangers."

"If only that was possible!" Miago said.

"The elders were very pleased with the symbol and there was much joy and celebration. To commemorate the event, a great painting was commissioned. The finest artists were put to work and they toiled night and day."

Miago was impatient to know the end of the story. "What happened to this painting and symbol?"

Thunder Fly leaned forward. "When the painting was finished Banakaloo-Piki grew jealous and she took her revenge with fire and thunder. She emptied the molten rock that fills her belly on this place, she turned day to night with clouds of ash that poisoned the land and the ocean. Many people were killed; the painting and symbol were lost."

"What happened to the Supreme Ruler's son?"

"They dug him out of the rubble. He was injured but alive. Then the evil ones came out of the forest and took control. They invited him to a meeting and murdered him."

"Are you saying," Miago spoke slowly, "that the Men of Knowledge ... are the evil ones?"

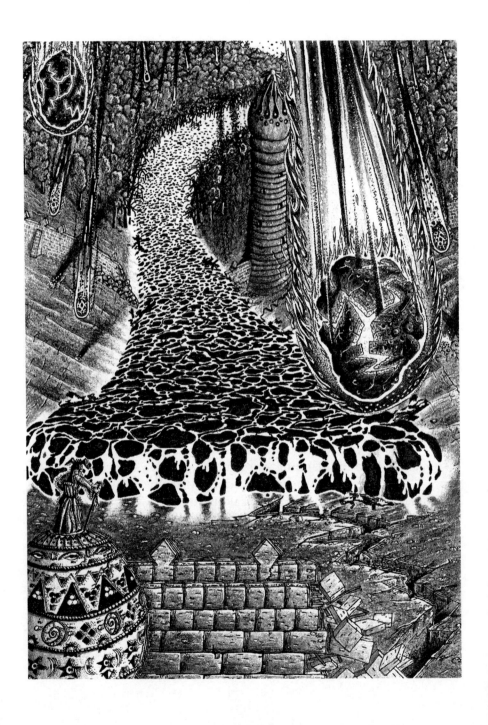

Miago's father ignored the question. "They say that a red orchid grows on the spot where he died ... beside a waterfall."

"So that's why they called themselves the Red Orchids," Miago said before adding, "but there's no waterfall near here. The closest one's at Vulture Pass."

His mother picked up the story. "They threw his body into the volcano and told the survivors he'd gone away."

Rain Dancer joined in. "They say the Supreme Ruler's son reappears sometimes."

Miago spun round. "When?"

"The legend is that he returns when we have an eclipse and stays until the next full moon."

"But we have just had an eclipse!" Miago shouted.

His mother's voice was filled with sorrow. "Still he does not come."

"He does not come because it's only a legend," Thunder Fly said flatly.

"You didn't answer my question." Miago said.

"Which question Mudskipper?"

"You admit that the Men of Knowledge are evil?" Miago asked, staring at his father.

"Son, there are so many stories that it's difficult to know what to believe. After all, it happened many years ago."

Miago was silent.

"But they do a good job. Perhaps their wisdom seems strange at times ..." Thunder Fly added weakly.

Rain Dancer nodded. "And it's better to ignore stories," she said kindly. "They only told you because it was your right to know. They told me when I was fifteen."

"We are all prisoners here," Miago said forcefully. "We are controlled in our minds and I don't know if I can live like this. What if the legends are true?" He was growing angry, "How can I make my Life Choice now? Maybe I won't!"

His mother gasped. "Swear you won't even consider the challenge of the caves. Swear it, Miago!"

Thunder Fly spoke. "My advice is, go to the shrine and kneel before the Sacred Emblem. Burn two, no, three herb bundles and breathe deeply. Then ask the Great Goddess to guide you. I'm sure she'll advise you to be a Worker, as we both wish."

He embraced Miago awkwardly. At first Miago squirmed but finally he tightened his grip across his father's back.

When Thunder Fly spoke again, his words were only for his son. "I know I can be a stubborn fool but I only do what I think is best. You are so important to me. I'm sorry if sometimes I seem ..." He sniffed. "I couldn't bear to lose you too." He was shaking now as the tears came.

There was a lump in Miago's throat. "No one blames you for what happened to Cufu," he said. As Miago saw his father's vulnerability, he recalled their other arguments. Had this vulnerability always been there? "I understand now," he said softly. "We all have to make choices in life. It's never easy."

The talking stopped and still they embraced. When they parted, they did so in silence. Miago managed a smile before he hugged his mother and sister. He kissed Thunder Fly and left the room. He had taken only a few steps when the question came: *so how much of the teachings do any of them believe?*

Miago entered the shrine, he struck the bell three times and waited until its piercing ring had died away. He lit the candle and the herb bundles; kneeling, he breathed the sweet-smelling fumes, concentrating on the Emblem of Penance, as he had done many times before. He closed his eyes to pray but he could only think of how his parents and sister lived their lives controlled by fear. He thought of the vision he'd had when swimming and the feeling of love, a feeling he hadn't experienced since Cufu's death. *Does life really have to be like this?* He remembered what the Chameleon had said about the importance of laughter. *There isn't much laughter around here.* Finally, there was Monkey Blood, loathed and ridiculed because he wouldn't conform. But there was something about him Miago had come to respect: his honesty.

Miago opened his eyes to see that the candle had burned down to its final flickers. There was a movement outside; he heard footsteps and the rustle of clothing. He rushed to the window and looked out, searching left and right before he saw it: keeping to the shadows, a cloaked figure darting from house to house.

Miago moved back so he wouldn't be seen. When he spoke, there was contempt in his voice. "Why were you spying on me?"

BLACK GOLD

The procession moved to the beat of a single drum. The children wore tunics of hessian belted with rope; in their right fists they clasped a small Emblem of Penance, their left hands were pressed against their hearts. Miago knew T'lu-i was three rows ahead because she kept turning to gaze at him. He couldn't smile so he looked down as his mind raced with unanswered questions. He thought of the Chameleon. Was he somewhere in the crowd? How much had he really helped? With so little time left, Miago's Life Choice seemed more difficult than ever.

Ahead was a stone dais on which stood a line of cloaked and hooded figures. Their cloaks matched the black slopes of the volcano that rose behind them. On one side an area had been cleared for celebration and Miago saw the fish, pigs and deer cooking on spits but the smell of food did nothing to dispel the nausea he had felt since morning. The women, dressed in their most colourful clothing, waited motionless beside urns of dizzy juice. But would it take away the pain?

Someone tugged Miago's sleeve and he turned. The man was shaved and clean, his hair looked washed, his clothes tidy. It was a moment before Miago recognized him. "Monkey Blood!"

"I wanted to say good luck. The most important thing? Be true to yourself, young man."

Monkey Blood was forced to dodge around bystanders as he struggled alongside Miago. "I have to live with my cowardice forever," he said. "The friends I betrayed. I know you are brave enough to make the right choice and, whatever happens, I will respect you for that."

"The friends you betrayed?" Miago asked as the procession neared the dais.

Monkey Blood was slowing. "There were eleven crosses on that knife," he called. "One … for each of us."

Miago stumbled with shock. "You mean the blood pact?" he said, twisting his head back, straining to keep Monkey Blood in view. "You were a Red Orchid?" The truth hit him. "Ten died in the caves but there are eleven crosses. You were the one who didn't go in, weren't you?"

Monkey Blood nodded slowly. "As I said before ... I died years ago."

A soldier pushed Monkey Blood away. "No talking now. You, boy, keep moving!"

Monkey Blood's eyes looked heavy. His head dropped in shame and his stooping form was swallowed by the crowd.

Miago was carried onward by the procession which halted in front of the dais. Miago swayed, and grabbed the boy next to him.

"You're about to become a man," he hissed. "Men don't faint!"

Miago steadied himself, breathing deeply. He looked up at the dais and at the hooded figures.

A Man of Knowledge raised his arms and turned to face the volcano. To Miago it seemed more menacing than ever and, as the speech started, his fist tightened on the emblem.

"We are gathered here on this special day in memory of our foolish ancestors and in the presence of our kind protector, the Goddess of Fire and Thunder, Banakaloo-Piki ..." At his signal everyone turned to face the Great Totem and, on a drumbeat, as one they bowed. They stayed like that until a second beat sounded. But Miago bowed less deeply than the others, and, instead of closing his eyes, he looked around him. *Are they all so afraid?* "... for our annual ceremony as decreed in your sacred teachings. We are grateful, Great Goddess, for your continued guidance and mercy and we will not flinch from our duty to correct our ways and learn from the mistakes of the Befores. We thank you for your generous decree that all men may carry knives for protection against the heathens who continue to steal our children and desecrate your sacred grasslands with their cattle."

The speaker turned to face the crowd. "This has been a difficult year but, citizens, you have done well. To keep you on the path of forgiveness, the Great Goddess has issued new decrees."

"What now?" Miago whispered.

Others were whispering too.

"The eclipse was indeed a sign!"

"At last our suffering will end!"

A girl near Miago spoke louder. "Will we be spared the marking?"

The Man of Knowledge was speaking again and the crowd fell silent. "Before I announce these, I have good news. The Great Goddess shares your pain when you go hungry. In her compassion she has chosen to reveal the secret to harvesting the ocean's unlimited bounty. You must mix twenty tarama leaves with a handful of seeds from the hanging fig. Cook them in coconut milk with the guts of two large blowfish. Mix with sand to make the mixture sink. One measure will fill a canoe with fish."

The shouting started immediately. "Thank you, Great Goddess!"

"So that's Six Toes' secret!"

"We won't go hungry again!"

"And now to the decrees! Firstly, the blacking of the temple has pleased the Great Goddess and next the Palace of Peace will be painted black. It is her wish that henceforth the temple will be known as Building One, and the Palace of Peace as Building Two."

A wave of muttering rolled through the crowd.

"Second, any man or woman who has made their Life Choice will from tomorrow wear a hood in public."

Some of the soldiers had drawn their swords; others were shouting: "Back in line!" "Silence!"

One pointed at Miago. "Eyes front, boy!"

That makes no sense, Miago thought. It will hide the marks. He remembered the Chameleon's words that most people chose one of the three paths anyway. Perhaps the brandings weren't really so important after all.

"These hoods must be black." The Man of Knowledge looked around before continuing. "The situation will be reviewed at the next ceremony."

Then he raised his hand and slowly the muttering stopped.

"We have arranged sufficient supplies of black dye which can be bought in the market."

"Black gold!" Miago hissed. "So that's how you'll make more money, Market Man. Black buildings, black clothes. Where will it end?"

The Man of Knowledge was speaking again, "And now I have more good news. To reward you for your efforts, it is decreed that each year a number of exceptional citizens will be chosen to travel. They will be charged with spreading our truths to distant peoples and they will bring glory to this place as others adopt our ways. They will receive great rewards for being in the vanguard of what in time will become an army of believers as person by person, village by village, tribe by tribe, the world is converted to our ways."

The Man of Knowledge waited as a fresh wave of whispering washed through the crowd. When it had subsided, he spoke again. "There are those beyond our walls who would harm us. You know about the Moroks but there are others in distant lands who are also evil. So our citizens will be disguised. They will receive special training and they will be known as the *Unseen*. There will be no need to hide when our truths have spread to all people."

Miago looked around at the mass of stunned faces. Even the whispering had stopped.

"Your Men of Knowledge have agreed that one citizen has earned the honour of being appointed the first *Unseen*." He paused. "This man is a credit to this place and those who wish to follow in his footsteps should follow his example. His name is …" he let the tension build. "Market Man!"

"It *would* be him!"

"He'll return even richer."

"How can he hide with a leg like that?" someone mocked.

"I might want to be rich," Miago whispered, "but I'd never sink that low."

The Man of Knowledge bowed to the volcano. He sat down as a second Man of Knowledge stood to address the crowd.

"This year we bring before you, Great Goddess, these young adults who are in their fifteenth year ..."

Miago looked around expecting to see shock and defiance. Instead, he found blank acceptance. *What's wrong with them?* Somewhere deep inside, Miago felt the stirrings of a decision. In that moment he desperately wanted to find his family, to smile at them and feel their love but a soldier moved forward and jabbed him on the arm. "Eyes front, boy!"

"Let the ceremony begin!"

A young girl stepped forward and knelt. She raised her head. Miago saw the metal handles that protruded from the licking flames of the brazier. A Man of Knowledge called out the girl's name and shouted: "A Thinker." As the crowd applauded, the hooded figure lifted a brand, holding it high so the crowd could see its glowing end. The crowd stilled as the hooded figure advanced, brand extended. Miago heard it: a short hiss. The girl didn't flinch. Swaying, she rose slowly. A moment later she was waving. Flowers were thrown, people cheered.

But Miago was silent as a wave of disgust engulfed him. *I don't know if I can go through with this ...*

"Her adult name is Flower of Thought."

A woman stepped forward and dabbed the burn with paste. She placed a garland of tropical roses over the girl's head and she was led to the area cleared for celebration. Her family burst from the crowd to surround and hug her.

Damago was next. In the silence Miago willed a beam of courage his way.

"A Believer!" bellowed the Man of Knowledge as Damago knelt and raised his chin.

But when the glowing brand was almost on him, Damago panicked. With a cry he leapt back. He was shoved forward by the boy behind him, seized by the guards and forced down. The brand hovered above him. It came down and Damago's head rolled and jerked as he fought desperately to avoid it. There was a hiss and Damago screamed. With a moan he slumped over.

The Man of Knowledge prodded Damago's foot with the brand. There was another hiss. "This foolish boy resisted and moved his head. As a result the mark is … unsatisfactory. He will carry this as a reminder all his life. Let that be a lesson to those who come next. He'll receive no numbing paste nor will he partake in our celebrations. Henceforth he will be known as …"

There was a deathly silence as the crowd awaited the decision.

"Dog Spit."

Miago saw Damago's tears and how the skin had tightened around the burn. He tried to catch his eye, to offer him some reassurance as the guards dragged him, shaking and sobbing, away.

"I swear, cousin, the day will never come when I use that name," Miago whispered as his fist opened and the emblem fell to the ground.

A hush fell on the crowd as the ceremony continued and others were branded. Miago felt strangely detached as they knelt, their names were called and, line by line, he moved closer to the dais. His mouth was dry because now T'lu-i was kneeling before the Men of Knowledge. She spun around, her pleading eyes wide with uncertainty. He knew she wanted reassurance and that his smile looked forced. He saw her lithe beauty, her perfect skin; and he thought of what they were about to do to her. He felt desperation and a great sadness that she had chosen this path rather than face the caves because together they might have stood a chance. If only he had spent more time talking to her, trying to explain; perhaps if she'd come to know the Chameleon … but now she was about to be disfigured. He couldn't watch.

"A Worker!"

"I won't warn you again, boy. Eyes front!"

Miago turned back slowly. He winced as the glowing brand stilled above her. He saw her vulnerability but he ignored it to relive her smile, her laughter and the scent of flowers. He sought refuge in his most precious memory – the night in the forest. With a sob, Miago closed his eyes.

When it came, the hiss seemed to go on and on, filling his head, screaming through his brain in a bolt of white-hot energy. Gasping, Miago staggered as he tried to cover his ears; groaning he opened his eyes. From somewhere, he found strength.

The children who surrounded him retreated from his energy as he stood tall, tensing every muscle in his body. The single word flew at the dais and at the line of hooded figures: "NO!"

For seconds it boomed around the square. When silence returned, heads turned. From far away, Miago heard the voices.

"What has the fool done?"

"They'll throw him in prison for that!"

Aghast, T'lu-i turned to face him and he saw the angry, swelling burn. "Why, Miago?" she cried. "Why?"

She was sobbing but all Miago could see was her beauty and something exquisite in her tears. Because finally he knew that she loved him.

In that moment he was grabbed and thrust forward. The soldiers dragged him to the dais where the scent of charred flesh hung heavy in the air. Dizzy with fear, Miago looked up but even the natural light failed to reveal the hooded faces. "So, boy, it is you! You dare to interrupt the ceremony?"

Miago didn't know what to say but unchosen words tumbled from his mouth: "I want to take the challenge of the Caves of Blindness!"

There was stunned silence. Miago felt a hand slip into his and a reassuring squeeze. He looked into T'lu-i's eyes and she let him go much deeper than before. As he stared he saw the oozing burn, her pain and their stolen future.

"Be brave, Miago," she sobbed. "Be brave and come back to me."

There was a crack on Miago's head and he fell. Stars flashed around him as they dragged him away; he coughed and chocked, twisting to protect himself. Something sharp gashed his elbow but he felt no pain. Finally he bounced down stone steps, landing with a crash on his shoulder. He heard the clunk of bolts, a muffled laugh, then silence.

LISTEN AND OBEY

With a groan, Miago pushed himself up and looked around. The room was small and cold, the door reinforced. A shaft of evening light entered through a window barred with iron; the walls and floor were stone.

The shape in the corner stirred.

"I was wondering if you would be joining me."

Miago gasped. "What are you –?"

He never finished the question. The Chameleon's clothes were ripped and stained. One eye was swollen shut. A gash split the eyebrow where the blood had dried black. Miago saw the gap left by a missing tooth. The pouch still hung from the leather belt but the shells had been smashed. He was cradling a piece of timber that had been roughly carved into a bowl. The coconut-husk hat lay shredded around him.

Miago's voice cracked, "What have they done to you?"

The Chameleon smiled. "Nothing."

"But your teeth, your eye!" Miago was staring now. "Your eye looks terrible! It looks … have they blinded you?"

The Chameleon gave a strange smile. "Ah but I have two left."

Miago moaned. "Two? How can you talk in riddles at a time like this?"

The Chameleon laughed and slapped his thigh but he flinched as a bolt of pain racked his face.

"Why do you laugh when I know you suffer?"

The Chameleon sighed. "Is pain so important? What is an eye or a tooth? They would have to go so much deeper to hurt me." He picked up the carved shape and placed it on his head. "A perfect fit."

"I told you a wooden helmet wouldn't protect you," Miago said in exasperation.

The Chameleon took it off. "It's not a helmet," he said.

"I had hoped to finish it on this visit." He looked at the boy. "I can guess why you are here and I am proud of you."

Miago laughed bitterly.

"You are the only brave one in your year. You deserve to feel good about that. Sit up, shoulders back. Breathe deeply. How does that feel?"

Miago did as he was instructed. "Fantastic," he said sarcastically.

"Hmm," the Chameleon said frowning. "I suppose it will take time. Now, tell me, what happened to T'lu-i?"

Miago sighed deeply.

"I see." The Chameleon looked up. "And how did you feel when they branded her?"

"I ... " Miago looked down. "That's why I'm here."

The Chameleon sighed. "I will have to give this some thought. The problem is that I am leaving tomorrow."

"They're throwing you out?"

"Not exactly," the Chameleon replied. "You see, they told me I had broken their laws and the penalty is death."

Miago gasped. "They can't kill you!"

The Chameleon chuckled. "You are right. They can't kill me because I will be long gone."

"Long gone? How will you get out of here?"

The Chameleon only smiled.

"Where'll you go?"

"Home."

Miago hesitated before asking his next question. "Where's home?"

"We've had this conversation before but we have more important things to talk about, like your problems. First I have a question. The other night I heard you caught a Morok, or Quma as I prefer to call them. But he escaped. Is that the whole story?"

"Not really." Miago lowered his voice, "I let him go."

"Your sworn enemy and you freed him?"

"When I saw him, he wasn't the monster I'd expected. He was only a man, a small, frightened man. And, and ... he talked of *tocamu*."

"Ah, *that* one. He is a good man."

"But Mongoose and Blowfish were sent after him. They were told not to return without him."

"In which case they will still be searching for him." The Chameleon said.

"Why do you say that?"

"That Quma is no fool. He would have left false trails. They won't catch him."

Miago frowned.

"What's troubling you?"

"There was something else about the Quma," he added uncertainly. "He said his people never take our children."

"You believed him?" the Chameleon asked.

"First I was told the rain fever killed Cufu. Then that the Moroks – I mean the Quma – took him. But the Men of Knowledge knew the name of Cufu's possum. How could they, unless Cufu told them? Which means ..." he was whispering now, "*they* took him ..."

A memory came and he trembled as he spoke. "When I climbed the tower with T'lu-i ... we saw a Man of Knowledge wrapping something. He set off for the volcano with it. The next morning I was in the Great Chamber and there was a woman screaming outside. Her child had been taken in the night."

Miago sprang up and ran to the wall, hammering it with his fists. "They call themselves Men of Knowledge?" he screamed.

"Oh, they have knowledge," the Chameleon said coldly.

Miago turned to face the Chameleon, his fists were still clenched as his chest rose and fell. "Is this the truth?" he whispered. "Tell me! Do I finally know the truth?"

The Chameleon's sighed deeply. "I'm so sorry Miago, I'm afraid that finally you do. The Men of Knowledge sacrifice children to the volcano and blame the Quma. They only do it when the Quma are camped on the plain to make everyone think ..." his voice trailed off.

Miago sank to his knees. The Chameleon placed a hand on his shoulder. "Let it out, Miago," he said gently.

Blind with tears, shaking with rage, Miago jumped up and rushed to the door, banging on it with his fists. The guard shouted angrily, "If you don't shut up, I'll come in there and –"

"What else can you do to me?" Miago screamed. "Come in and kill me, come on! I don't care!"

Miago sank to the floor, sobbing. Minutes passed as the Chameleon watched and waited. Miago was fighting against accepting the truth: *how could they do that to Cufu?* His body stiffened as he raged at the murdering Men of Knowledge. "Those deceitful, murdering, lying pigs! No wonder they hide their faces!" Finally Miago forced himself upright and spoke, struggling to control his voice.

"I think I worked it out the other night. I just couldn't admit it. But, *why?*"

The Chameleon's voice was level. "Because hating others makes it easy to forget about our own failings. Oh, they're very clever and I fear they are winning." When he spoke again, his tone had changed. "But they haven't won *yet*. Now, Miago, tomorrow you must challenge the Guardians. And remember – you only need defeat one of them."

"I've been thinking about that," Miago said slowly. "Is that because, by defeating one, you defeat them all? It's about the way you defeat them that matters."

"I'm pleased with you!" the Chameleon smiled. "But remember, if you fail to get past the Guardians, you cannot return to the village."

Miago nodded. "I know. I must kill myself."

"Don't be ridiculous! That would be a waste of a young life and would mean they had won. Worse still, I would be very upset!"

"What choice would I have?"

"You could go away, start a new life somewhere else. As I've told you before, the world is a very big place, Miago."

"You don't understand," he tried to explain. "The most important things are here – my family, T'lu-i. I must survive the caves and return to the village. I must!"

The Chameleon remained silent. Eventually Miago spoke again. "My mother said the cave traps are based on the mistakes

people make in life."

"That would make sense."

"Do you know what those mistakes are?"

"My advice is pay great attention to how each test makes you feel."

"I think I understand."

"But now you must sleep. I hope you can get comfortable."

Miago lay down.

The Chameleon smiled. "Good luck my friend, and try to remember everything we've talked about."

Miago shifted and turned on the stone floor and it was some time before he slept. When he did, he dreamed of the volcano and the Guardians. His dream shifted to slow, drifting shapes in the forbidding depths of the ocean. The Chameleon stayed awake. He spoke softly to Miago until his dreams changed and he was with T'lu-i, splashing and laughing in the foaming surf.

When the Chameleon saw that Miago's fluttering eyes were joined by a smile, he opened his pouch and poured the contents onto the floor – pieces of broken triton, pebbles, a small bone and a leaf. The Chameleon sorted through them until he found what he wanted. He picked up the toucan feather and gently stroked it back into shape. He held it up and prayed, and placed it on the sleeping boy's forehead. He sighed. "I am glad you've found some peace in your dreams. Killing the shark was a test that proved you are closer to understanding than you think. Miago, you can defeat a Guardian." The man studied the boy closely. Finally he whispered, "When you are in the caves, you must listen and obey."

Miago was woken by a kick.

"Where is he?" Termite screamed.

Miago spun round but the cell was empty. "I, I don't know!" he said in amazement.

"How did he escape?" The guard shook him, his face slack with fear.

"I don't know," Miago insisted. "He was here when I fell asleep."

Termite drew his sword. "You'll tell me or you'll die!"

The blade was level with Miago's belly. He retreated until his back was pressed against the wall. He pulled his stomach in as far as he could. "If you kill me, you'll only get into more trouble!"

"You are correct, boy."

The voice had a dry rasp that Miago recognized. Mesmerized, he stared at the hooded figure as the Man of Knowledge entered the cell. The man tapped the walls. "Solid stone." He looked up at the skylight and tested the window bars. He ran his fingers along the metal strips that spanned the timber door. He even fiddled with the bolts.

"Was this locked?" he snapped at the trembling guard.

"Yes, sir, top and bottom!"

"And the sentries?"

"Awake all night, as you ordered. I swear it, sir!"

"You should try something for that snoring, Termite," Miago suggested helpfully.

The soldier stiffened and his eyes narrowed. "You'll regret that remark, boy!" he snarled.

"So my suspicions were correct and again he escapes," the Man of Knowledge said thoughtfully, pacing the cell. "But he has done little harm."

He turned to the guard. "You will escort the boy to the Painted Rock. You will ensure he makes his prayers there. The Guardians are expecting him."

Termite bowed and left the cell.

The hood and the man it concealed held a terrible fascination for Miago. He was trembling as the idea came to him. Breathing deeply, he remembered Cufu. Was this the one who had taken him? Had Cufu seen his face before he died?

"Why are you staring at me, boy?"

Miago stepped forward as if to leave the cell but he was

concentrating on the hood. His hand flashed up and grabbed the coarse cloth. With a yank he pulled it back.

Many times Miago had lain awake thinking about the Men of Knowledge. He'd let his imagination run riot, creating toothless old men with wispy hair, grey spirit faces that the light passed through, dry skulls with empty eye sockets and even reptile-skinned Moroks. When he added eyes, they were yellowed slits, webbed with broken veins; if there were teeth, they were stained, non-human stumps. In his dreams Miago had met cloaked corpses and poxed ghouls, faces blistered by fire and withered by disease. Sometimes he'd constructed entire monsters like man-bats, or creatures that combined the demons of land and sea. But Miago now stood transfixed, icy fingers closing around his heart. Because he had recognized the face. It was his own.

Miago struggled to free himself from the mocking stare that held him. He could hear the thumping of his heart and knew he should run. The spell was finally broken by the Man of Knowledge's bone-dry laugh. Tearing his eyes away, Miago leapt outside and sprinted past Termite. He knew this had to be some kind of magic and that if he believed it, it would take his mind. Maybe they'd slipped something in his mouth while he slept. He was sweating heavily as he ran, but it was a cold sweat and, when the face stole back into his thoughts, he shivered. Chest heaving, Miago slowed at the edge of the forest. He leaned against a tree to catch his breath.

He heard cursing that grew louder as Termite appeared. The soldier spat on the ground and wiped his forehead. He prodded Miago's leg with his sword. "Don't try running again!" he warned. "Or I'll slash your tendons ... what do I care if you crawl to the volcano?"

They walked in silence deeper into the forest. The track snaked upwards and at first Miago refused to look at the volcano but as they climbed, he glanced at the craggy peak and curling smoke. Below it barren rock filtered into scrubby vegetation. Miago knew the caves were where the trees thinned and he shuddered when they rounded a bend. Because ahead lay the Painted Rock.

Termite forced Miago down with his sword. "Now make your final prayers," he ordered.

Miago knelt and as thoughts raced through his mind, he heard a distant voice.

"I'm leaving now. Enjoy your death." Termite laughed and Miago heard his steps fade to silence.

When Miago stood, he found himself alone in a silent forest. The mist had cleared from the entrance to the caves to reveal a jagged hole. His stomach lurched: it resembled the jaws of the shark.

He took a few steps back and gazed down at the village. "T'lu-i, I love you," he said as he searched for her house. "Somehow I'm going to survive and come for you."

After a prayer for his family, Miago took a deep breath. Slowly he turned to face the caves.

DOESN'T THAT TASTE GOOD?

There was little to see and it was strangely still – there were no animals or insects, Miago heard no birdsong. No *life*. The air felt thick, as it did before a storm, and he breathed it slowly as he edged closer to the caves. Peering into the black entrance he heard a distant rumble that seemed to rise from the very bowels of the earth. It was followed by a tremor and he dropped to his knees in fear. *The Goddess knows I'm here and she's angry.* A crack of thunder made him jump back; now there was movement as whirling specks of light danced inside the caves. Fireflies? But the lights merged to form three distinct shapes. Miago heard the tramping of feet and that was when he realized he was looking at the Guardians.

Their eyes were locked on him, and their expressions oozed contempt. The one on the left was as round as he was tall. Miago saw how his soft body quivered like jelly; that the muscles had wasted to pitted, concave strips. His limbs were bowed, wisps of hair struggled to cover the pear-shaped head. The wobbling belly looked ready to split open and let the fat inside pour out. A pendant hung below the double chin. Its shape told Miago that this revolting creature was the Thinker Guardian and the eyes, darting and calculating, confirmed it.

The Worker Guardian's pendant bounced like a trinket on the matted hair of his chest. His flat nose, vast nostrils and sloping forehead reminded Miago of a jungle gorilla. Unlike a gorilla, Miago saw the blaze of anger in his black eyes. The oversized head rested on a wedge of muscle that extended to his ears. Bulging and quivering, the vast chest met the enormous arms in a series of humps and dips; the bone-hard stomach was sectioned into incised squares. The black body hair had knotted into curls and, where flesh showed through, Miago saw thick, purple veins. When he looked closer, Miago saw that the anger was mixed with enduring stupidity.

The Believer Guardian was an impossibly thin creature of bone and sinew who reminded Miago of a stick insect. He could count his ribs; he saw how they were fused to the breastbone because there was no muscle, only a thin covering of translucent skin. His tangled hair met an equally tangled beard that flowed down to a pigeon chest. As if weightless, he glided forward. His eyes were bathed in a deep serenity that fitted neither the time nor the place.

Miago's instinct was to retreat, to turn and run, but he forced himself to hold his ground. The Guardians stopped in front of their enemy. One of them spoke.

"We wait and wait and this is all they send us?" the Thinker Guardian asked. "You, boy, you think you can come up here and challenge our authority? You dare question the wisdom of your Men of Knowledge?"

Miago hardly dared lift his face as a wave of futility swept through him. He hadn't expected them to be so large, so confident. So threatening.

The Worker Guardian flexed his muscles and rolled his eyes. He spat on the ground. "Grrrrrrrrrr, let me go first!"

"No," the Believer Guardian snapped. "Wait your turn!" He studied Miago. "This one has no chance of defeating us. Look at him. He trembles like a leaf!"

"Looks like he may be about to cry!" the Worker Guardian taunted.

"Stay upwind," the Thinker Guardian added. "I think he may have an accident."

The laughter that followed was a hideous mixture of roars, squeaks and guffaws. Through it, Miago could hear the thumping of his heart. Though he wanted to turn and run, he was frozen to the spot.

The Thinker Guardian stared long and hard at Miago. "So boy," he sneered, "I spend all day thinking. I have answers to everything. So how do you propose to defeat me?"

Miago repeated the question and scratched his head. His quivering voice betrayed his fear. "Well, I ..."

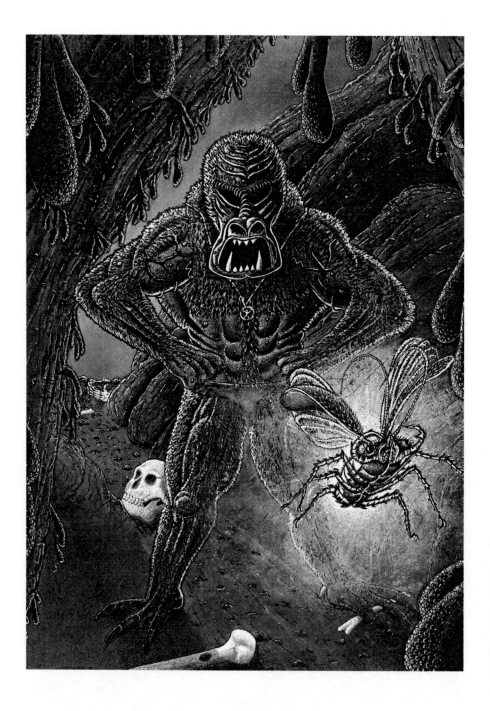

"You can't answer my simple question but you have the arrogance to think you can survive in the caves?"

With hopeless certainty, Miago knew he could never defeat the Worker Guardian. He shivered just thinking about him. "But I can't argue with you," he said in desperation. "You know too much."

The Thinker Guardian yawned. "Of course I do!"

The Worker Guardian roared with delight. He interlocked his fingers and flexed his huge back, the vertebrae clicking one after another. He cocked an arm and studied his veined bicep. It was bigger than Miago's head.

"Young fool," the Thinker Guardian mocked. "I knew you would fail my test." He winked at the Believer Guardian. "Your turn!"

The Believer Guardian was staring blankly at Miago and he seemed to be filled with a contentment that Miago found both confusing and irritating. Boredom filled his voice when finally he spoke. "I am attuned to my spirituality; I know my gods and they love me."

Miago waited for more but instead the Guardian closed his eyes and prayed.

"But that wasn't a question!" Miago finally said.

"Who said anything about questions?" bellowed the Worker Guardian.

The Believer Guardian stood quite still, a grin spreading across his face.

"So how can I win?" Miago asked in desperation.

"You can't," smirked the Believer Guardian, "because I believe and nothing can shake my belief. There is no question, only my answer."

"But you can't have an answer without a question. That's not fair!"

"Who said anything about fairness?" the Thinker Guardian taunted. He turned to the Believer Guardian. "Did you?"

"No."

"Did you say it would be fair?" he asked the Worker Guardian who tried to look intelligent. "Let me think. No, no, I don't believe so." His eyes narrowed. "My turn!" he snarled.

Miago was turning to run as the huge shape bounded forward. With a leap the monster was on him. He crashed down and the air was crushed from his lungs. The Guardian thrust the boy's face into the dirt. Miago was choking but now his head was wrenched over. The Guardian squealed with delight as he slammed him down again. Spasms shook Miago's body. He kicked his legs and flailed his arms but the pressure only increased. He tried to pull free but a giant hand clamped around his throat and he was lifted and shaken, then dangled at arm's length. Miago clenched his fist and swung at the ugly head, putting all his strength into the blow but his arms were too short and he missed. The Guardian lifted Miago higher, spinning him above his head. With a roar he was hurled to the ground.

Miago pretended to be knocked out but it made no difference: he was dragged up by his hair and punched in the stomach. Doubling over, his head collided with the hairy foot that shot up to meet it. Miago threw his arms around the leg to stop another kick but a ridge of knuckles smashed into his neck and he slumped to the ground. Feebly he tried to avoid the next blow but the huge foot had settled under his ribcage. Bleary-eyed he looked up at the towering shape it was attached to. He heard a sadistic laugh as the foot jerked up and then, "Bye bye!"

Miago let himself roll, hoping to put as much distance between him and the Guardians as possible but he smashed into a tree stump and everything went black.

Dimly, through the pain, Miago heard voices.

"That was too easy."

"No fun at all."

He stayed very still, hoping his spinning head would clear.

The Thinker Guardian prodded him. "He dared believe he could argue with *me*!" As one, the Guardians roared with laughter.

Carefully Miago opened his eyes.

"Oh, look!" said the Believer Guardian. "He wakes."

"You can't sneak back to the village now," the Worker Guardian taunted. "So eat those," he said, pointing at a cluster of mushrooms. "Then I'll hurl your corpse into the volcano!"

The mushrooms were brown and Miago saw that tiny insects crawled over them.

"Go on, eat and prepare to meet your maker," the Thinker Guardian said.

Miago had let everyone down. His body was racked by pain, he knew he had failed. The fight had been kicked out of him and there was nothing more he could do. He reached out and grasped a handful of mushrooms; they felt slimy and cool. *Please kill me quickly.* He put one in his mouth and began chewing. It tasted bitter and his mouth flooded with saliva. He was about to swallow when a tiny caterpillar fell into his palm. Lazily he studied it as a memory was joined by an idea.

"Doesn't that taste good?" growled the Worker Guardian.

But Miago was playing back the Thinker Guardian's words: meet your maker. What had he learned from the Chameleon about strength? What had killing the shark taught him? He spat out the mushroom and placed the caterpillar gently on a leaf. "I hope we both become butterflies," he whispered. He drew in a deep breath and forced himself to think. When Miago spoke, he tried to sound confident.

"Where were we, gentlemen?"

The Worker Guardian's eyes narrowed. "You want a second chance? I won't be so gentle this time!"

Miago looked at the Guardians in turn before addressing the Believer Guardian. "You, weren't you the one who said something about spirituality?"

"Yes. My gods love me."

Miago kept icy calm. "Your gods love you, do they? But look at you!" He pointed. "My sister could lift that rock. Could you?" He stared at the Guardian's puny arms. "Why, you couldn't beat my mother arm wrestling!"

Miago's remarks were met with silence. Growing bolder,

"As for intelligence, I bet you couldn't win an argument with ..." he pointed, "that stump."

"Is there more?" the Guardian asked.

At least they'd stopped taunting him and was there a little ... hesitation in the Guardian's voice? Miago thought carefully. "Your gods gave you three gifts. Like my miserable people who know only suffering, you all ignore two of them."

"What would those gifts be?" the Worker Guardian asked carefully.

"Your bodies, your minds and your spirits." He saw the look that passed between them.

"Where is this leading?" the Thinker Guardian asked.

"I think ... they all must be combined."

"Indeed? What would happen then?" asked the Believer Guardian.

Miago was struggling to make sense but the words began to flow. "If someone did this, his suffering would end. As more people did the same, families, cities, even tribes, would begin to enjoy life. People would learn to live in peace with themselves and with all mankind." He looked at them in turn. "The ancients called this *tocamu*."

As Miago stood, he wondered whether he'd got it right. When the Thinker Guardian finally spoke, the menace had left his voice.

"I congratulate you, young man. I never thought you would earn the right to enter the caves but sadly you have achieved nothing because, like the others, you will certainly perish in them."

The Believer Guardian sighed. "Another wasted life."

The Worker Guardian surprised Miago. "I hope I didn't hurt you too much," he said. "Hurting people is what I am commanded to do."

The Guardians formed a line again but, strangely, they now looked smaller.

"We must give you these," said the Thinker Guardian. They removed their pendants and hung them around Miago's neck.

"There's something else," the Believer Guardian added.

"You must remove your clothes."

"Go in there naked?" Miago asked warily. "Why?"

"If you are successful you will discover the reason," the Believer Guardian replied. "If not …" He shrugged.

The Worker Guardian handed Miago a torch of bound sticks. "This will light your way."

Miago peered into the entrance to the caves. He saw two openings. "Why are there two tunnels?" he asked.

"The caves consist of a series of tunnels that link chambers," explained the Thinker Guardian. "You must choose a tunnel and then pass through into a chamber. Survive a challenge and move onto the next …"

"The left tunnel is for those who are here because they are failures back in the village," the Believer Guardian said. "They may hate themselves or have no self-respect."

The Worker Guardian pointed to the right entrance. "That one is for people who feel good about defeating us. They realize how clever they have been or they are good at something and enjoy the feeling that brings. The choice is yours."

Miago was proud he'd defeated the Guardians and he knew he was the best shell collector in the village. He thought of T'lu-i, the most beautiful girl of his year, and how she'd chosen him. "I hope all the challenges are as easy as this one!" he said, as he walked boldly towards the right tunnel.

SLIPPING SILVER

As Miago stepped into the tunnel, the temperature dropped and the scents of the forest gave way to a stale, damp smell. Ferns bearded the roof, the walls were mottled with lichens. Moving slowly to allow his eyes to adjust, he felt spongy moss underfoot. From the darkness came the distant drip-drip of water. Had he glanced behind him, he might have seen the cloaked and hooded figure that emerged from the shadows to follow him.

Miago forced himself to use his senses. He studied the shapes and textures and controlled his fear when he couldn't see into the blackness. Concentrating on the smells and shadows, straining his ears for clues, he moved on as every step took him deeper into the volcano.

He came to a patch of crusted yellow wall. An acrid odour seeped into his lungs and burned his eyes. He held his breath and moved faster to find clean air and soon he was running. Just as the passage began to dip, the floor smoothed to slate. He was struggling to keep his balance when he hit a patch of slime. He crashed down and scrabbled for grip but it was no good – as the slope increased, he slid faster and faster. He shouted in desperation, holding the torch high as he snatched at the wall but it too was covered in slime. Stubby plant roots hung from the ceiling and, though he lunged for them, they were beyond his desperately grasping hand.

Rushing towards him, Miago saw something hanging down. Another root? A length of rope? He knew he had to grab it to stop his momentum so he raised his hand and concentrated on the target. He would need all his strength but he would not miss.

Something is wrong! As the warning shot through him he pulled his hand down and threw his head to one side. He turned and, with a surge of disgust, he saw it was the rusting metal of a sword blade.

Miago's speed was building. He tried digging his heels in but on he tumbled until he flew off the end of the tunnel and crashed in a cloud of dust. The fall winded him and when he could breathe, he coughed and spluttered. Carefully he stretched his limbs as, bruised and disoriented, he waited for the dizziness to pass.

He clamped a hand over his nose as the dust settled, rejoicing that the torch still burned. Soon he could make out shapes. With horror he realized they were bones and that his elbow was resting on a skull. When he saw the deep gash where the sword had split it, he said a prayer for its victim. With a tremble he whispered, "The Guardians aren't playing games."

Miago heard a noise. He strained his senses, tilting his head to hear more clearly. It sounded like scratching and seemed close. A mouse? Beside him lay a femur; carefully he lifted it. The bone was light and dry. The noise stopped so Miago shook it and something rattled inside. There was scratching as tiny claws struggled for grip. As a wave of revulsion swept through him, Miago hurled the bone to the ground because mice didn't rattle.

He fumbled for a weapon, his eyes locked on the bone. *Be brave, Miago, kill it!* He was lifting a rock when an amber shape emerged, antennae circling above the shiny head. He struck hard but he was fooled by its speed. Pivoting, he struck again, catching the insect across the back. "Die, you revolting bone beetle!" he shouted in triumph.

Miago expected to see an explosion of browns and yellows. Instead, the beetle lay crushed in the dirt. He nudged it, ready to strike again. He tapped its back. One leg twitched and straightened. Then another. Now the antennae were moving again as the beetle sprung upright. With a jump it was facing him. It spat.

Miago jerked his head away, clamping his eyes shut as he threw an arm up in defence. When he looked again, he saw armoured plates open and stubby wings unfold. Lit by bioluminescent patches, the beetle lifted clumsily into the air.

A fizzing drone filled the cavern as it clattered against a wall.

It bounced off to fly into solid rock once more. Miago smiled at its stupidity as it closed on a darker patch of wall where it settled and the light went out. He thought of walking over to smash it to pieces but he knew he had more important things to do. "I pray that's the last beetle I see in here," he whispered.

Miago stood to get a better impression of the chamber. It was larger than he'd thought and the uneven walls threw long shadows that shifted in the torchlight. What lay on the floor made him gasp.

In places the bones were jumbled together, so he started by counting the skulls. He saw that some people had died by the sword, one skull had even been cleaved in two. But what had killed the others? Perhaps they'd lost their torches and had stumbled in the dark until they starved to death? Maybe they'd been drained of blood by vampire bats or blinded by beetle spit?

Now he saw that the walls were speckled with insects and, when he got closer, he knew what they were. "Cave flies," he whispered. With disgust he pictured their writhing maggots that reduced flesh to syrup. Shuddering, he remembered the noise he'd made when he'd crashed onto the chamber floor. Was a giant snake now slithering his way?

It was dangerous to stop moving, fatal to waste time but Miago could find no exit. He worked his way around the cavern, checking behind a shoulder of rock. He studied the walls and ceiling, remembering the stories he'd heard of the dozens who'd died in here. There weren't enough skulls so there must be a way out.

He stopped where the bone beetle had landed. The wall there was so thick with flies that they covered the rock. He wondered whether they were hiding a door so he thrust the torch at them. Only a few took off so he drove the flames into their midst and, with a buzzing roar, they lifted to swarm around him. Through the cloud of metallic green, Miago saw scratch marks that looked like writing. He made out the words:

> As deeper in these caves you go,
> Your demons better you will know.
> The fool ignores his darker side
> With eyes in which the light has died.
> Before the hostage's behest,
> Your inner wars must come to rest.
> Remember what you seek you find …
> To find your way, unlock your mind.

"Another riddle," he moaned. He was reading it again when a fly landed on his lip. He slapped at it but with a scurry it ran up his nose.

He tried to blow it out but it clung on; when he breathed in, it crawled deeper. It was now tickling the back of his throat and, doubling over, he coughed and spat. He guessed it wanted to lay eggs there and desperately he coughed again. Now it was on the back of his tongue and he gagged. It flew out in a ball of spit and he stamped on it, hard. He looked up at the writing and read it again. Somehow he knew it was important, but what did it mean? With a shrug he turned away.

He was back at the entrance again and on an impulse he raised the torch to light the tunnel's walls. Some way up he saw an opening. A way out? Excited, Miago climbed into the tunnel but the slime offered no grip and he slid back into the chamber.

He tried again, this time moving slowly, digging his nails in, only to slip back again. He ran at it, diving up the tunnel, scrabbling for grip but it made no difference.

"I defeated the Guardians, I dodged the sword, only to die in here ..." he groaned as he sank to his knees. His despair turned to anger. Jumping up, he slammed his fist into the wall until the skin was red and broken. "You fool!" he shouted. "You didn't have to do this! See where your stupidity's got you! You should have taken the other tunnel!"

Miago grabbed a handful of dirt and hurled it across the cavern. He threw more until the air filled with dust. He smashed a dried ribcage against the wall. He was about to throw the torch after it when an idea came to him. He stood thinking it through as the dust and his anger settled.

One-handed, Miago threw the dirt into the tunnel so that it covered the slime. It wasn't fast enough so he wedged the torch in a crevice and used both hands. He worked hard and he ignored the pain: *keep going, Miago, show no weakness!* He pulled himself onto the dirt carpet. Yes, he had grip! He grabbed the torch and worked his way up the tunnel until he came to the opening. He crawled in.

The new tunnel twisted and descended and the roof was rising. Crouching he moved forward, soon he could stand upright. He hurried on, knowing his life depended on how long the torch burned. He stepped over a small ridge and ducked beneath an overhang where the tunnel split. Uncertain which way to go, Miago pushed the torch into the right opening which swelled into a mud-walled cavern. He examined the left side. What sort of test was this?

Miago noticed the wall in the left chamber was paler in colour, and his attention wandered when a noise drifted to him from its depths. For a moment he wondered if it was the tinkle of running water, or even a twisting wind lifting dried leaves. But as the noise grew, he became certain – it was singing.

It was a voice of such range that Miago couldn't tell whether it belonged to a man or woman. There were no words or pauses for breath – only a seamless flow of notes that swirled around him.

So precise was their pitch, so clear their tone that they might have been carved in crystal. Now the music was bouncing off the walls to duplicate itself in a synchronised echo that split again and again until the cavern rang to the most beautiful music Miago had ever heard. His only thought was how he had always wanted to sing and so, wide-eyed, he stepped forward. He noticed the air here was cooler and how good it felt on his sweating skin; he paid less attention to something that brushed his foot, only glancing at the dark, hairy shape. A dead rat?

He hadn't moved far but he felt short of breath. A few more steps brought him closer to the singing that still burst around him in a cascade of harmonies but, strangely, the torch had dimmed. He put his tightening lungs down to excitement as he edged forward in search of the gift of song.

But now Miago's breathing grew even heavier until, stooping, he was struggling for air. When he thrust the torch forward, the flames barely flickered. A few more steps and the torch had all but died. His thoughts returned to the music and, swaying, he pleaded into the blackness, "Will you teach me to sing?"

"Come closer, Mudskipper."

Miago gasped. He was trembling when he forced out the word: "Mother?"

He laughed at his change of fortune, he thrilled as he imagined his new voice. "I didn't know you could sing like that!"

"There's much you don't know about me."

"Teach me!" he begged, "and help me find my way out of these caves!"

"So come closer Mudskipper ..."

Miago stepped forward, his arms outstretched, into a cloud of warm, damp air. He stopped suddenly, gagging because the smell was imprinted on his memory. He saw again the vultures thrusting their heads into the caged corpses that hung beneath the Great Totem. It was the rotting stench of death.

Miago leapt back. The strength was gone from his voice when he pleaded, "Mother, is that really you?"

Had the torch grown brighter? He noticed the shape on the ground. Again he saw the dark, knotted hair. He flipped it over with his foot. It was no rat. In the half-light he made out the bulging eyes and withered tongue. The mouth was toothless, locked open in a silent scream. Trembling, he prodded the shrunken head to feel the softness of the skin. When he saw the delicate eyelashes he moaned, retreating until his back struck the cave wall. Now the flames leapt and crackled. He backed towards the fork, stepping over more shrunken heads. A voice broke the silence. "Come back, Miago, and I will teach you to sing ..." But now there was something new – a shiver of menace. He pushed the torch out but still there was blackness. Something glinted beside him and Miago knew he must look. He turned to see that the mud wall was patterned with enamel; it wasn't the word he read that made him gasp but what formed the letters: human teeth.

With a cry he retreated until he found fresh air. He asked himself how the caves had known of his desire to sing and why he had heard his mother's voice. And why did the mosaic spell ENVY?

A screaming howl burst behind him and he ran. It crashed down the tunnel in a pressure wave that struck him like a fist. The terror drove him on. Wide-eyed, too scared to turn, he prayed he wasn't being chased. My god, he thought, what sort of demon was that?

Miago was still sprinting; the path was straight and level. But there was silence and, when finally he dared turn, he could see nothing. He slowed to a jog as the walls narrowed, their constriction forcing him to walk. He squeezed forward but in time the tunnel split. The left fork was bare but the right wall had been smoothed and polished. On it he saw neatly written names arranged in columns. He began reading. "The ones they branded," he whispered with contempt. He saw there were more names at the foot of the wall. The letters here were cruder; there were splashes of ink and places where it trickled onto the floor. "You could have shown some respect," he bellowed. "Monkey Blood and Damago are my friends!"

He moved on until he found his parents' names. He stroked the letters gently. "What would life have been like without the barbaric ceremony?" As he recognized more names, more memories came and his anger grew.

Miago found Rain Dancer's name. There was Hard Hands … now he paused because he'd come to his year. Though he saw that the writing had stopped, the wall continued on into the darkness. "So this is how you keep score, is it? And I see you're expecting more," he hissed.

He read the final name: T'lu-i. Miago pounded the wall. He held the torch up until a layer of soot coated the letters. "I'll die before they list you," he sobbed as he stepped into a new tunnel. What he saw there stopped him dead.

The latticed ironwork and protruding brands were unchanged and as he stared, his anger rose. When he approached the brazier he saw there was a large hole beside it in the tunnel floor. He bent forward but the torchlight was lost on its plunging sides. He grasped the brazier and with horror found it was still warm. Flexing his muscles, he prepared to hurl it down the hole. "Damago, T'lu-i, at least some good will come from this!" he raged.

With his fury came a memory: the fighting fisherman and the Chameleon's advice about controlling your anger. He let go and stepped behind the brazier. Why was the sand not level? He brushed it with his foot to reveal a thick rope, one end of which was knotted to the ironwork. He followed it to a crevice in the wall. It ended overhead, bound to stout planking. Through the gaps in the timbers he saw the boulders they supported.

Miago retreated from the imaginary rockfall. Smiling, he walked back. One by one he lifted the branding irons, spitting on each in turn. With a roar of triumph he hurled them down the hole. "You didn't think of that, did you?" he shouted. He waited and listened but he heard no impact.

He ran on, unaware of the distance he was covering until he reached another fork, one side of which was blocked by a fall of rock. As he steadied his breathing, he became aware of a noise. It was a buzzing that came from behind him. Looking back, he saw nothing. He raised the torch; ahead, he saw how the stones matched the surrounding walls. A natural rockfall?

They were heavy and jagged; why waste time clearing them? He heard the buzzing again and spun round. Far behind, a light hovered in the gloom. "Why are you following me beetle?" he asked. *Stop wasting time Miago!* He turned and jogged into the clear tunnel.

The new tunnel took him deeper into the volcano. Where it levelled, the silence was broken by the drip-drip of water. His foot struck something. The torch lit a stony lump that grew from the floor. He came to another that reached to his knee. Raising the torch, Miago saw that there were more overhead that grew in length and number.

The texture of the floor now changed. With his next step, Miago smelled a sickly sweetness. It grew stronger and, breathing through his mouth now, he stepped forward. The crust gave way and he sank ankle-deep into something cool and gritty. A stench erupted around him. Gagging, he drove himself forward, feeling the oozing softness that worked between his toes.

His progress slowed. Moments later he was knee-deep. Though the air was cool, Miago was pouring with sweat as his revulsion mounted. Exhausted, he stopped to rest. *What is this?* Then he prayed it wouldn't get deeper.

He looked down at where his blackened legs disappeared into the rotten-smelling gunk. It was filled with seeds and in places it moved. He gagged when he saw the pulsing grubs that worked it. Praying for solid rock, he lurched ahead until finally he dragged his legs free. He ripped handfuls of slime from the walls and tried to wipe himself clean but it made no difference. He retched at the smell, and now his legs were tingling. Would it burn his skin?

Ahead something shimmered. Miago lifted the torch, and, with delight, he saw the flame reflected in water. His spirits soared – he could wash! Rushing to the edge, his eyes fell on a mass of blue-green crystals deep beneath the surface. Their colour was soothing, their size extraordinary. He imagined selling them from T'lu-i's stall but the thought brought a wave of pain. Would he ever see her again?

He ducked when a flash of light buzzed over his head and

splashed into the water. In an instant the wings had folded and stubby legs propelled the insect into the depths. He lost it under a rock overhang. "You can swim, can you? Well I hope you drown!"

Now he saw that the depression opened into another water-filled chamber. It was larger and Miago noticed the detritus that drifted in the current. He studied a finger-sized shape that spun and twisted. He was watching a transparent shrimp, barely visible but for the black line of its guts. Another movement caught Miago's eye as a fish emerged from beneath the overhang. Instead of swimming, it walked inverted on the rockface, working its fins like legs. It left the overhang and swam towards the shrimp. Fascinated, Miago pushed the torch forward as the fish closed on the shrimp.

It was unlike any fish Miago had seen. Large scales ran into stumpy fins and the body ended in an ugly head from which jutted long fangs. A gulp and the shrimp was taken. The fish turned and slipped beneath the rock face.

"I'm sorry, shrimp," his voice echoed strangely in the chamber, "I didn't think it would catch you because … it had no eyes."

If shrimps and fish lived here, the water couldn't be poisonous. Miago thought of climbing in and swimming until he was clean. Did he have time? And if the pool had small fish, maybe there were bigger ones that ate *them*?

Miago balanced the torch and leaned forward to scoop up handfuls of water. He soaked his face and shoulders before washing his body.

He heard a clicking. Lifting the torch, Miago stared at where the ceiling changed from grey to black. A wing, all skin and bone, unfolded from a hairy body. Miago froze when he realized what were hanging above him in their thousands: bats.

He gulped in air; a scream was coming and he was losing control. Could they smell him or sense the warmth of his body? With a surge of nausea he now understood what he'd been wading through.

A noise made him turn. A zephyr rippled the water's surface

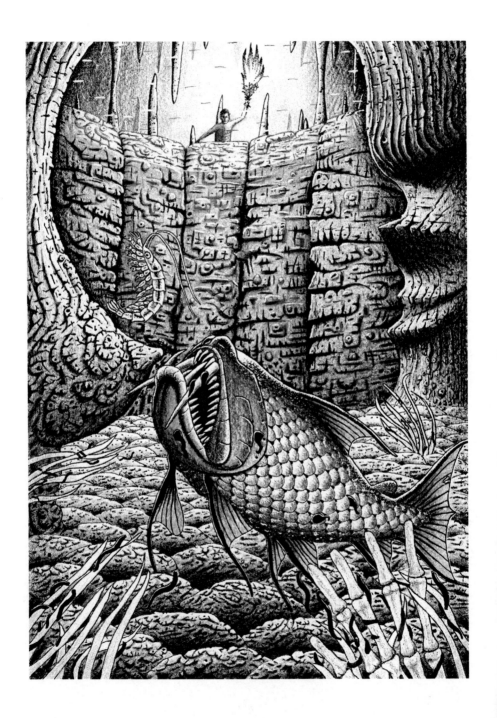

and he liked the way it brushed his body. He was less sure about the cold feeling that tickled his spine. He knew he should move on but, strangely, something held him.

As he watched, he wondered if the water level was rising, and if there was more debris. He saw leaves and twigs, weed and slime, and now the water was turning a milky white. He saw the beginnings of a whirlpool that seemed to be pulling everything into a single mass.

He moved closer as the twigs and leaves formed a shape in the twisting spiral. As he was drawn to it, a doubt began to play on his mind. *I thought you only got whirlpools when water flows out.*

Miago saw how the clumps of weed had anchored to a rock that was rising from the depths and how thin and delicate they'd become. *So rocks float here, and water flows backwards?* He tilted his head because, from that angle, the rock almost resembled a face. Yes, something about the play of light and shadow gave it eyes, and even a nose. And that crease that seemed to be opening looked like … a mouth.

The pool was close to overflowing. Miago was transfixed by the spinning water as he studied the shape materializing before him. At first he tried to deny it but the components had come together and the shape was complete. He blinked and stared; he told himself it wasn't possible because he was looking at a woman who was fashioned from the secret elements of his deepest longings.

He'd known this strange reality before. Sometimes she came on the hottest, most humid nights when he drifted in and out of sleep. As in those half-dreams, there was something about forbidden excitement and the knowledge that no one would know.

Her soft hair fell around a face of alabaster. Her eyes, wide and pleading, reached into his mind and seeded it with images of their shared need.

In her body, Miago saw an exaggerated T'lu-i that mocked her perfection. He saw fuller, redder lips that contrasted with cloud-white teeth and darker eyes that shone even from the water.

At first Miago felt a warmth that told him he was blushing. Other feelings arrived and the heat moved lower. Bolder now, he stared at her body and at the way the current stroked it. Something pulled his eyes down to the kink of her hips and to a dark stain where the weed grew thick and tangled. So when the woman smiled, Miago smiled back. When she questioned him, he answered.

Somehow, he heard his name.

He heard more: she told him his place was with her, that alone he could never defeat the caves. Breathing heavily into her words, she said how long she'd waited for him. As ripples of pleasure coursed through his tightening body, her textures and scents, and the promise of immortality reached from the water and claimed him.

In a dream, Miago edged forward. Dropping the torch, he prepared to climb in but with the flames no longer lighting the pool, he lost her and the spell was broken. For seconds he stood staring into the semi-blackness as slowly, his mind cleared. He stepped closer, hoping to see her again but the water that at first seemed to draw back, now bulged and trembled. It rose and rose, pushed by an unseen form that was level with his chest, then his head, now it towered above him. Miago was struck by a wave of malevolent energy that sent him reeling backwards. He tripped as something monstrous erupted from the pool, sabre teeth flashing in the half-light. He saw a scaled body, lit with flashes of light. There was the vague outline of a head, a knotted mane of hair. For seconds the demon, part woman, part fish balanced on the sweeps of a giant tail as it searched for him. Then the jaws clattered shut and with a showering splash, it was gone.

Heart pounding, Miago saw that by some miracle the torch still burned. His legs at first betrayed him so he crawled on his belly. Shivering, he seized the torch. Willing strength into his legs, he jumped up and fled. And as the light cast a final beam across the pool, a small, eyeless fish settled again beneath the rock overhang.

Miago sprinted down the tunnel. He fell but he was quickly up and running again. He banged into a column, yelping as he caught his elbow. Rounding a corner he burst through a cloud of midges, their tiny bodies pasting his sweat-soaked skin. Something croaked nearby as he charged through a mist that made the torch smoke and spit. He pushed himself on, knowing he must put as much distance between him and the water as possible. When finally he felt it was safe, he leaned against a wall to steady his breathing.

There was sand ahead and as he moved forward, it thickened. A few more steps and he raised the torch, forcing his eyes to see into the gloom. Had something glinted? His heart was hammering as he moved faster because he remembered the stories of treasure. He stumbled into a run and with every step the object became clearer. It was gold!

It was crudely fashioned and no bigger than his finger but he knew its worth. Clasping the ingot firmly, he edged on in search of more gold. A second ingot protruded from a crack in the wall and, as he seized it, his battered spirits soared.

There, on a bank of slime lay another. Then he found two together. Lifting the torch, Miago thrilled to see that the passage ahead was littered with gold.

He held five but he needed more. In his nakedness, there was only one option – by abandoning the torch he was able to form a pouch with his hands and scoop up more ingots.

The next bend revealed more gold and he collected it quickly. Little light fell there and he moved now as much by feel as by sight, stooping under the weight of his load. Complete darkness brought a moment of unease but moments later he spotted a chink of light ahead. Clutching his treasure, he whooped his delight as he closed on the exit.

His first thought was of the house he would buy – one of the good ones that stood beyond the reach of the lava. He laughed wildly. He could buy two or three and he'd still have more money than he could spend in a lifetime! He giggled in triumph. *Now who's rich, Market Man?* He'd get his own canoes and pay boys to collect shells. Or he might buy one of the trading boats with the triangular sails that handled the roughest seas. In time he'd own a fleet. Though his back had stiffened and his legs ached, he was laughing as he stumbled towards his new life.

It was as if an unseen hand blocked him. He was so close but he stopped and he thought. Even when he heard the squeaks and he knew that rats were coming, he stood his ground.

Every muscle told him to try to outrun them but he bit his lip and braced himself. There weren't many at first, but the vanguard thickened into a plague of scrabbling, slick bodies that raced down the passage. It was a soft, writhing carpet that flowed past shin-deep but instead of running he closed his eyes and fought against his growing revulsion. He kept telling himself to be strong – this had to be the final test.

Just when he thought he'd break, when he saw himself sprinting over them, as he imagined his feet crushing their warm bodies, their numbers eased. As quickly as they'd arrived, the roar of scratching, squeaking rats had moved past. He opened his eyes. There were stragglers and one sniffed his leg. It scampered over his foot and he felt the brush of its tail before it plopped onto the sand.

Moments later, he heard it: far behind there was laughter.

But instead of hurrying on, Miago paused because questions now crowded his mind. Had he really been that clever finding the gold? If so many people had died in the caves, why weren't there more skeletons? Some of them must have found the treasure so why hadn't they returned to the village? And why was he naked?

Miago put down the gold. He felt the pendants that hung on top of each other, tracing the shapes of the Worker, the Believer and the Thinker. The images, branded on his memory since childhood, popped into his mind. That was when he heard the first clicks.

Miago stiffened as he imagined one bat after another dropping from the cave walls to hover and circle as their number grew; the coppery-red bodies, the foaming, bloody mouths.

He thought of running but instead he dropped as they whooshed overhead. Soon he was crouching under the stream of clicking, flapping shapes, fanned by countless skin-covered wings. He looked up when the last bat had passed. "Ha!" he shouted.

"Was *that* the final test?"

Miago groped his way back to the torch, praying it hadn't gone out. With joy he saw that it still glowed faintly. He blew on it, coaxing it back to life. Finally a flame came, then another.

He caught his breath. The torchlight revealed his footprints but also a second set that had come this far, then turned back up the tunnel. He lifted the torch that barely penetrated the gloom. But way back, he saw a patch of light blink out on the tunnel wall. "Whatever evil magic you are using, I'm still alive," Miago said dryly into the darkness.

He ran back to where he'd left the gold. When he reached it he inched forward, checking his footing with every step. Without warning, the path opened into a cavernous hole. Looking down, he saw the broken bodies impaled on the bamboo spears and the ingots that surrounded them. "So many made that mistake," he gasped as, shaking with relief, he asked himself how much gold he really needed.

The torch was close to dying. Miago ripped off the pendants and threw them into the pit. "Guardians, you can come and get your trinkets!" he shouted, picking up two ingots. He inched around the pit and ran.

He sprinted until he came to a fissure that opened by his foot. It started as a small crack but grew wider with every step. Soon it was deep enough to hide a man. Now the crack had grown into a channel and the channel into a gorge and as Miago advanced, he wondered how he'd cross.

He jogged on as the passage curved and dipped until he was rewarded with a sight that at first thrilled him – ahead was a tunnel entrance from which radiated a glow of light. But his joy was short-lived because the gorge was spanned by a rope bridge and he didn't like the way it sagged. Up close he saw that the ropes were frayed and the timbers rotten. It was obviously a trap, but Miago could see no other way to cross. He glanced back but he knew he couldn't retrace his steps so he stood where he was, searching for ideas.

He peered into the gorge to gauge its depth. It was deep enough. He noticed a series of handholds on his side but the opposite wall was smooth. It made no sense until he imagined the breaking bridge and the tumbling victim. Of course – the handholds allowed the Guardians to recover the pendants. As he paced and fretted, the overhead shadows danced in the torchlight.

Miago was moving back when he found the first bone. Another step brought more: a skull, and beyond it, a pelvis. He knelt to pick up a handful of ribs, his finger tracing the cracks that split them. He was surrounded by death, but what had killed these people? Why were the ribs broken and why were they so white? He stopped to search for answers. Overhead the shadows stilled with him. Except for one.

The great shape was darker than the surrounding rock; black chevrons decorated the scaly body. Unblinking eyes were fixed on Miago as the monstrous serpent slid forward to settle in a mass of coils above him.

Miago stared blankly at the bridge as the serpent's flicking tongue tasted the air around him. The neck pulled back to form an "S". Too late Miago felt the specks of sand dislodged by its rippling body.

The great snake struck in an explosion of power, battering Miago on the shoulder and knocking the torch and the ingots away as it threw coil after coil around him. Writhing frantically, he fell to his knees amid the echoes of his own screams. His arms were pinned and, as the snake tightened its grip, Miago felt the air being crushed from his body. The pressure was bursting his ribs and he was unable to fill his lungs. Paralysed with terror, eyes bulging, he felt a coil move up to his shoulders. If it locked around his neck, he'd be dead in seconds. He forced his chin down and braced it there but, as he twisted his head sideways to breathe, the snake tightened its grip again.

He needed to do something, anything, while he still had air in his lungs. The snake was patient and seemed to be conserving its strength. Miago exhaled but, as his diaphragm contracted, the coils tightened once more. He tried to writhe, to free an arm. He opened his mouth and bit down until his jaw ached but the wall of muscle beneath the scales was as hard as iron.

Soon he would black out and the snake would constrict

again as it crushed the life from him. The ghastly jaws would open and dislocate to engulf his head, then his shoulders ...

They were close to the edge of the gorge. Leaning back, he felt the way the snake tensed to keep him upright. In that moment he used its strength as he flung himself forward. He pushed with his legs and together they toppled over the edge, striking the wall before the numbing impact of the cavern floor hurtled up to meet them.

When his senses returned, Miago found he could breathe and, though the perspective was new, the scene was familiar. He was floating above a rope bridge that scanned a gorge but this bridge looked strong.

Deep in the gorge, lay a shape as still as death. He saw a boy's legs protruding from a coiled mass, but in this dream state the scene had only a distant, detached meaning.

Miago liked the way the pain had melted away as he drifted into another tunnel. Here he felt great calmness as the faintest wash of silver built into a soft glow that back-lit distant shapes. At first they seemed to be part of the light but, as some of the shadowy figures waited, others now glided forward. Miago could tell they were people, spirit people; he saw men and women, a few children too.

An old woman advanced. With her, hand in hand, came a child wrapped in shimmering bandages. Miago's memory stirred. With joy he let the child draw him in so he floated towards the boy's outstretched arms. His throat tightened as he whispered, "Cufu." And, as they grew closer, Miago felt the love that still bound them. "We won't be separated again," Miago whispered.

But from afar a voice spoke. It carried command and it told Miago he should not be here. Cufu seemed to hear it too because his arms were dropping and he was pulling back. Miago willed him to stay but, even as he faded, Cufu spoke, "You must obey, Miago. But Cufu keep promise and help brother again."

Images of his loved ones filled Miago's mind. He saw his grieving family, then T'lu-i staring seaward, bathed in shadow by a cascade of boulders. When he allowed himself to picture the

Chameleon's face, he felt a charge of strength that flooded his whole body. Miago was told to make a final effort and he knew he must do as the Chameleon commanded. Then the tunnel dissolved in a cloud of sparkles.

Miago drifted like a clump of weed in a midnight ocean. When he glanced up, the surface was lost in the dimmest flickerings of light; below, the seabed merged with the formless black of the abyss. Lost and uncertain, he was trapped between worlds.

He never saw it coming, but the shape that shot from the gloom twisted around him. He heard the clicks and saw the laughter in the nodding head. The young dolphin stopped in a stream of bubbles to tell him they must do this together. Miago reached out and gripped its fin. It took him down.

The conch glowed silver on the sand. There was profound stillness and unbroken silence as his fingers closed around it.

With a gasp, he filled his lungs and opened his eyes. This time the coils didn't tighten. Writhing and twisting, he untangled himself from the snake; coughing and choking, he rolled away. He dragged himself to the foot of the gorge and found the handholds.

When Miago reached the top, he collapsed and stayed where he was until his breathing steadied. He flinched from the pain in his ribs, cursing his stupidity for hesitating at the bridge. Of course they'd make it look unsafe.

He crawled forward and retrieved the torch and ingots before stumbling across the bridge, which swayed and creaked. When he glanced into the gorge, the snake was gone.

Miago was in a new tunnel and every step brought more light. It ended at a set of rough-hewn steps that opened onto a domed chamber. He stood very still as his eyes were drawn to a waterfall. It was a great waterfall but not one of those mountain torrents, more a slipping sheet that from some angles shone like glass, and Miago could see the golden disk of the sun, the emerald of the forest and the tones of blue that were the ocean beyond. From another angle he saw a silver mirror and it was from this angle that he approached. When he was close, he stopped and studied his reflection. It was easy to see the Miago of old: the person he presented to the world.

He turned to see how the light fell on the wall behind. To his astonishment, he found that the rock was decorated from floor to ceiling with images that were as intricate as they were beautiful. The Great Painting! There was the old civilization with its pink temple and magnificent palace; people dressed in the finest clothing walked streets paved with stone. In the school, laughing children looked up at their smiling teacher. There was a vast fruit market, and another where richly woven rugs were displayed by strange looking foreigners. Beyond them Miago saw the fish market where the taku-aura were piled high.

The volcano was there and above it a dozen falcons held station in the thermals. The ocean was an electric blue; the bay was crowded with exotic vessels that squatted under the weight of their cargoes. He saw the canoes that ferried the cargoes ashore and a hundred more resting on the beach.

Miago followed the mural beyond the volcano to where the landscape was split by a river. Herds of cattle were tended by men on white horses; spirals of jewellery hung from their ears. His own people mixed with the Quma and, when he looked again at the market, he saw more Quma carrying fish and shells, sponges and coral back to a camp of brightly coloured tents.

On the highest piece of wall, the refracted light lit another scene that was framed in gold. It was of a palace that seemed to be perched on the roof of the world, so precipitous were the mountains that supported it, so thick were the clouds that veiled its spires. Miago frowned when he saw how the clouds powdered the jagged peaks with white, wondering why the rock wasn't black like the slopes of the volcano. He followed the peaks down to valleys split by rocky streams that swelled and merged to form great rivers. Where the rolling hills gave way to plains, the rivers slowed to meandering curves; beyond, the landscape wore the mantle of rainforest. He looked across the water where he found a ribbon of remote cliffs; above them dark seabirds wheeled. Higher still, swelling storm clouds reached with bulbous fingers for the heavens. "I didn't know there was land there," he whispered.

He was astonished by the painting and he wondered at how much of the world was unknown to him. He thought about the people who lived in the mountains or beside the rivers. What strange customs did they adopt? Which gods did they worship?

He looked up at the palace again and at a long hall where men sat at a table. Miago marvelled at the way the painted windows lit them with shafted rainbows because he had never seen windows do that to light.

Studying each man in turn, Miago admired their bright clothes and jewellery. They wore wooden crowns that were shaped like animals. There was an owl and a snake, a wild pig and a jungle cat. But Miago forgot the animals as he gazed at one man who was dressed like an emperor or king, and his mother's words came back to him. He was looking at the Supreme Ruler. He sat on a mahogany throne inlaid with oyster shell and gold, smiling proudly at a young man who knelt before him. The Supreme Ruler's crown peaked in three points from which burst colourful plumage. Miago recognized peacock, scarlet ibis and jungle cock and below them, a splash of emerald from the breast of a hummingbird. Rising proudly above these feathers he saw a spray of black and white tail filaments that came from the rarest of them all: the bird of paradise.

A great gem occupied much of the man's forehead, scattering its brightness like a million drops of rain. When Miago moved, the gem flashed and he saw now that it was not part of the painting, but stood proud of the wall. Miago froze when he realized that the gem was his for the taking and that its value was beyond measure. Without thinking, he traced its shape on his own forehead.

Miago returned to the kneeling figure in front of the Supreme Ruler and to the bird-shaped crown beside him. He knew the bird in an instant because its wings were black as night, its chest mixed white with yellow and the head finished in a colossal bill that glowed orange like the dawn sun.

The man's arms were outstretched and he held a cushion upon which something rested. Miago couldn't see any detail but he remembered the story of the symbol that revealed the truth

to peace and happiness; a truth that every power in his world had contrived to hide.

Miago's gaze returned to the kneeling figure. With a quickening heart, he aged him and dressed his chin with stubble. Then he gave him a stick, clad him in a cotton garment and a hat of coconut husk. As he recognized his friend, he felt the warmth of a tear that ran down his cheek.

Not expecting an answer, Miago asked himself how he felt. But an answer was waiting and it told him that the fears and questions that had stalked him since childhood, that had invaded his waking life and haunted his sleep, had abandoned their disguise to reveal themselves as ... friends.

Miago studied the painting until every detail was burned on his memory. He closed his eyes. When he opened them again, he found himself staring at a small chest. Why hadn't he seen it before? He stepped forward and picked it up.

The lid was polished tortoiseshell. He saw that the front and sides held familiar symbols: the *to*, *ca* and *mu*. The back was decorated with the butterfly symbol the Maker had drawn. His fingers told him there was carving on the base, so carefully he turned it over.

"Eyes?" he asked.

Holding his breath, he slowly raised the lid. The symbol rested on a piece of parchment; for minutes he stared at it. Finally he lifted it to reveal the writing beneath:

As the ground trembles and black smoke lifts from the volcano, we know our end is near. Though our time has come, we leave this symbol to guide and unite those who come after us.

Miago's fingers were clamped around the symbol as he replaced the box. He turned back to the waterfall. A final look at his reflection made him start because the bone beetle now hovered at his shoulder. He spun round but the insect was gone. In its place, black and hooded, stood a Man of Knowledge. "Who … or what are you?" Miago asked, controlling the tremor in his voice.

The shape was as still as it was silent. Miago continued, his voice gaining in confidence. "I finally understand what these caves are – it's what the Chameleon talked about: I was searching in the wrong place for answers. These caves are my mind and now I've looked inside myself. That's why the last part of the symbol is eyes."

Miago turned to face the waterfall again where the beetle, fainter now, was still reflected. "I don't fear you," he said and as he stared at its fading image, his voice was strong: "It's you that men blindly follow in life and more and more are adopting your ways. T'lu-i's grandmother called you her visitor but you go by many names. You are clever but now that I know you, I can defeat you."

Miago stepped forward into the gushing water, tasting its sweetness as it washed him clean. He stood there unmoving, blinded by the foaming bubbles, with the terror of the caves behind him and a new world in front.

Another step and he was through the water that returned in a blink to the sheet of slipping silver. He smelt the scents of the forest that mixed with the salt in the air and he felt the light breeze on his body. He accepted his nakedness because it reminded him of his place in the world and, as the drops dried on his skin, the chill carried a message about a new beginning.

The view, though familiar, was also strangely new. He gazed at the brightness of the sky and at the endless shades of green in the plant canopy. He saw as many tones of blue overhead and he followed them to where they merged in the haze of the horizon. A change of perspective and a macaw burst from shadow to dance its iridescence on the jungle's canvas.

He curled his toes over the cliff edge to watch the aquamarine ocean that rose and fell against the rock face to its gurgling heartbeat. Something unlocked inside him and he stretched until his back was straight and his chest pushed forward. For minutes he stood that way, filling and emptying his lungs. Wet from the mist of the waterfall, he found a mossy spot and lay down. He closed his eyes and where he lay, he slept.

When Miago woke, he did so slowly. If he had dreamed, it was forgotten. As he yawned he realized he had important decisions to make.

He stared out at the ribbon of white that was the reef, and beyond it at the cloud that hung over Offal Rock. He listened to the waterfall. Below, the water cascaded onto rocks before snaking across the bay. But the water that had once run clear was now stained red.

Through a chink in the foliage Miago picked out the golden sand and the scattered boulders that told him he was above Turtle Bay. As his eyes moved from shadow to sunlight, he saw the dark shapes that played there. Running, jumping, huddling together, the monkeys' chattering grew to a scream.

"What have you stolen this time, Pirate?" Miago asked fondly.

There were more screams and the monkeys scattered back into the forest. Then silence. But something looked different: a line of fresh footprints that worked their way towards the boulders.

One of the rocks had a new outline. As his focus improved, he could see the delicate profile and the way T'lu-i's hair shivered in the breeze.

He tried to shout but no sound came. Perhaps he would surprise her – he'd cut back into the forest and sneak up behind her. Maybe he'd tickle her but he dismissed these thoughts because they were the actions of a child.

T'lu-i's hands were buried in her hair as she sat there. Her body shook as her sobbing floated to him on the wind. Suddenly she tensed and stilled. Slowly she turned and she found him.

Their eyes met and they stayed that way, trapped in the power of that stare. The forest shared their magic as the chattering shapes came down from the trees to play on the boulders once more. The monkeys were young and they were curious; soon they had gathered around her.

He remembered the scratched writing and he repeated the words quietly to himself:

> As deeper in these caves you go,
> Your demons better you will know.
> The fool ignores his darker side
> With eyes in which the light has died.
> Before the hostage's behest,
> Your inner wars must come to rest.
> Remember what you seek you find ...
> To find your way, unlock your mind.

Lifting the ingots and symbol, Miago glanced back at the caves but the exit was now hidden by mist. He moved to the cliff edge and raised his arms. "I'm coming, T'lu-i!" he called, and prepared to dive. At the last moment he was distracted by a butterfly whose darting flight carried it to a tall, delicate flower that stood by the waterfall. Miago had seen orchids before but this one was different. So, out of respect, he waited until the butterfly had settled among the petals. Then, with a prayer of thanks, he dived off.

T'lu-i was running as he swam to the beach. They met in the shallows, throwing themselves together.

"I can't believe it!" she sobbed, kissing him again and again. "You're alive!"

Laughing, Miago held her tightly, letting her closeness wash through him.

They stayed that way until she giggled, "Miago, you're naked!"

He dropped his hands to cover himself but changed his mind. "It doesn't matter," he said softly. He kissed her beside the burn on her forehead. When she flinched, he asked, "Does it hurt?"

"Not now," she smiled. "You're covered in cuts and bruises! Are *you* all right?"

"Don't squeeze me too hard. I think a rib is broken."

T'lu-i ran her fingers lightly over his chest. "My burn will heal," she said sadly. "But I'll always carry the scar and it serves me right." She looked up at the volcano. "Something very strange is going on," she added. "There's never been a waterfall or river here but there was a raging, red torrent under the stone bridge. Look, now the water's almost gone."

Sure enough, the waterfall had been replaced by dripping vegetation.

"It's the legend," Miago explained. "The forest was washing away some of his blood."

"Whose blood?" Then she remembered. "You mean the wise man they murdered? You're saying it's true?"

Miago smiled. "Yes and I know who he was. I'll explain later

226

but now we must decide what to do. We can't stay here, they might send soldiers."

"What are you carrying?" T'lu-i asked.

Miago opened one hand and showed her the gold. He opened the other. "I found gold," he said simply. "And I found treasure."

T'lu-i's eyes widened. "So, so, the stories about a special symbol are true!" She studied it carefully. "It's beautiful. A little scary too."

"It's meant to be."

"I've seen these shapes before, haven't I?"

"Yes."

She moved closer and placed her hands on his shoulders. "Take me away from this place, take me with you."

"It will be dangerous. When you go missing, they'll send Trackers." He hesitated, "And what about your father?"

T'lu-i swallowed. "Miago, I know about him. He works for them, doesn't he?"

He nodded. "Let me protect you. If we walk through the forest they could follow us. But we won't leave tracks if we swim."

"Swim?" she asked nervously. "Where to? And what about our families?"

"Mine will think I'm dead. When it's safe I'll contact them. But you ... we'll have to make it look as if you killed yourself." He picked up a palm leaf and started brushing the sand. "We have to hide my tracks or they'll know. And you should write something in the sand."

T'lu-i formed the letters with her foot, "I can't go on without you, Miago."

He nodded his approval. "We need to find somewhere we can hide for a while." He pointed out to sea. "We could go there. They won't send anyone to find us."

"Offal Rock? Are you mad?" T'lu-i gasped but he was already walking towards the water.

"Trust me," he called over his shoulder. "It will be perfect."

T'lu-i held back. "We'll never swim that far. And ... and the sharks ..."

Miago walked back and placed a finger on her lips. "Shhhhh.

The current will carry us there. It looks strong today and there won't be sharks."

"But there's no food or water there." He heard the fear in her voice. "Only hungry insects."

Miago kissed her into quietness. "That's what you've been told to believe," he said. "But I know differently now. You must trust me."

T'lu-i's eyes held his and he heard a new calmness in her

voice. "You seem so sure of yourself and ... I want to be with you." She looked at the bank of cloud that hung over the island. "You know something? There's always cloud there, so how does anyone know what the island's really like?"

Miago smiled. "The Chameleon would be proud of you because now you're asking questions!"

T'lu-i glanced up and down the beach before turning to him with an expression he hadn't seen before. She giggled and stepped out of her clothes. "It's a long swim," she said pertly. "I won't need these."

Beneath her bravado, Miago saw uncertainty but her eyes sparkled in the sunlight, and she was smiling. He cleared his throat, trying not to stare. "Leave your clothes by the writing."

He dropped the symbol on her crumpled dress.

"Shouldn't we take it? It's valuable."

Miago shook his head. "Better to leave it for others. Its value lies in its meaning and we can take that with us. Anyway, I don't want to hold it when I'm swimming." He paused. "We can't take the gold either," he added, pulling his arm back.

"No, don't!"

The ingots flashed skyward before thudding into the rocks.

"Something new for the monkeys to play with."

Walking backwards, he swept the sand down to the water's edge. He threw the palm in and watched the waves take it. "When someone finds the symbol, they'll understand. Maybe they'll follow us."

"What if a soldier finds it?" T'lu-i protested. "He might realize how important it is. He might guess I faked my death."

"I don't believe anyone who thinks about it will stay loyal to this place," Miago said slowly. "Someone will find it and show it to someone else and word will spread and you know what?"

"What?"

"The soldiers aren't all stupid. Some of them will start asking questions."

They swam together, keeping close. Miago kept turning to look at her.

"Are you staring at me, Miago?" she laughed.

"Yes!"

"Don't ever stop," she said quietly.

Soon they were past the shallows in the deepening water beyond the reef.

"See?" Miago said. "Look how fast the current is. It won't take too long. That's it. Long, slow strokes."

The ocean turned a darker blue as it carried them along. When they were halfway they trod water as they tried to make out the island's features.

"I can't see anything," T'lu-i fretted, her fears returning. "All that mist. But you can see where the water gets shallow. I hope there's a gap in the reef. What if there's no beach? They say it's nothing but jagged rocks."

Miago jabbed her playfully. "There'll be a perfect beach," he insisted. "Stop worrying!"

"Oh, Miago, how can you be so sure?"

He spoke with conviction. "Because they don't want us to go there. They've taught us from birth that the place is dangerous but I learned in the caves that everything we've be told is a lie. So I think it's a lie too."

"But what can be so special about a small island?"

"I don't know. We'll find out when we get there."

They swam in silence until T'lu-i pointed. "Look!" A fish rose from the crest of a wave to glide away on delicate wings. Another skimmed the surface and in moments a dozen more had joined them. "Flying fish," she laughed.

They came to a floating log. "We can hold on and rest," he suggested. They saw the barnacles and the weed that made it home. "Don't cut your hands," he warned.

"It must have been in the water a long time," she said. "I wonder where it came from. It has strange bark." She looked at her wrinkled fingers. "A bit like me!"

"Look!" Miago rubbed away some of the weed. "There's something carved on it."

"Names?" she asked.

"I don't know – it's in a different language." She heard his change of tone. "The person who carved this may not look like us or talk like us …" he studied the letters again, "but they can feel pain and fear and joy just as we do."

"Oh, Miago …"

"We'll have to swim from here or we'll drift past the island."

"Thank you, log! I needed that rest," she shouted as she pushed herself free. Rested, they swam strongly until she said, "It's getting shallower. I can see the bottom."

She slowed and pushed herself higher in the water, but the afternoon sun lit the reef and made her squint. "Why's it so bright?"

Miago checked the angle of the sun. "I don't know."

T'lu-i looked down and gasped. "Look, is that what I think it is?"

Miago tilted his head but it made no difference to the glare that rose from the seabed. He fought to control his voice. "Yes! Look! There's another over there …"

"And another," T'lu-i shouted with delight.

At first the conch shells were scattered, but now they were clustered in patches of silver that captured the evening sun and bounced it back to the surface. The patches thickened and as the water grew shallower, they saw that the shells were piled one on another to form a rising slope that brushed the surface.

"The island's surrounded by a reef of silver conchs!" Miago cried. "Look at them all! There must be millions!"

"Why have they all come here?" she whispered.

When they reached the glittering reef they climbed carefully until they stood on its burbling summit. Together they looked back at the volcano; from their vantage point it had lost its menace. Together they turned to plunge into the calm water.

"Look at all the fish!" T'lu-i lifted her hand and a small fish lay there, quite still. "They even let you pick them up." She released it and laughed as it swam beside her.

The change was so slight that at first they weren't sure it was happening. A crack appeared in the mist that grew until it let in the first beams of light and allowed them to glimpse the emerging shapes and colours.

The sand there was golden and it swept down to the water

in an unbroken crescent of velvet. Beyond the beach, a tumbling lushness spilled its tendrils onto the sand. They climbed from the water hand in hand.

Flexing her toes, T'lu-i whispered, "The sand's so soft." More thoughts came. "And there's so much vegetation. The trees … what type are they?" She didn't wait for an answer. "It's so peaceful, so … beautiful."

She pointed at something on the sand. "What's that? A giant coconut?"

At first, Miago thought it was a lump of driftwood, but there was something familiar about the knife marks where the wings were taking shape. He lifted it carefully.

"He never had time to finish it," he whispered.

"Who?" T'lu-i asked. "What is it?"

Miago stared up at the jungle. "It's a crown," he said at last.

T'lu-i looked surprised. "A crown? It must have been carried here by the current."

Miago's voice was very quiet. "I don't think so." He turned the crown over and his gaze fell on the toucan feather that was pinned to it. He blew gently on the feather, stroking it until he'd brushed away the sand and realigned its delicate filaments. He cradled the crown under his arm, taking care not to crush the feather. "So this is your home, my friend," he whispered. "A place that's near – but so far away."

T'lu-i's voice was growing in excitement. "I've never seen mangoes that size. And those berries! Look at those bananas and that tree. Are those figs?"

But Miago was deep in thought. "I have completed one journey and another begins," he said.

"What was that, Miago?"

He took her hand and led her towards a path littered with fallen fruit. And as they started along it, the island stirred as the birds and the butterflies and the animals of the forest moved from the shadows to greet them.

THE END

Author's Note

Thank you for reading *The Toucan Feather* which I hope very much you enjoyed. If you would like to find out more about the tocamu concept, please visit tocamu.com.

M Stafflitur

Nicholas Stafford-Deitsch
April 2010

Lightning Source UK Ltd.
Milton Keynes UK
12 July 2010

156899UK00009B/206/P